THE GREAT
GHOST HOAX

THE GREAT GHOST HOAX

Emily Ecton

art by David Mottram

 Atheneum Books for Young Readers
NEW YORK LONDON TORONTO SYDNEY NEW DELHI

atheneum

ATHENEUM BOOKS FOR YOUNG READERS

An imprint of Simon & Schuster Children's Publishing Division

1230 Avenue of the Americas, New York, New York 10020

ATHENEUM BOOKS FOR YOUNG READERS is a registered trademark of
Simon & Schuster, Inc. Atheneum logo is a trademark of Simon & Schuster, Inc.

For information about special discounts for bulk purchases, please contact Simon &
Schuster Special Sales at 1-866-506-1949 or business@simonandschuster.com.

The Simon & Schuster Speakers Bureau can bring authors to your live event.
For more information or to book an event, contact the Simon & Schuster
Speakers Bureau at 1-866-248-3049 or visit our website at www.simonspeakers.com.

The text for this book was set in Adobe Caslon Pro.

The illustrations for this book were rendered digitally.

Manufactured in the United States of America

0721 FFG

First Edition

2 4 6 8 10 9 7 5 3 1

Library of Congress Cataloging-in-Publication Data

Names: Ecton, Emily, author. | Mottram, Dave, illustrator.

Title: The great ghost hoax / Emily Ecton ; illustrated by David Mottram.

Description: First edition. | New York : Atheneum Books for Young Readers, [2021] |
Audience: Ages 8 to 12. | Summary: When Mrs. Third Floor visits and reports paranormal
activity on the fifth floor, Butterbean and the other pets set out to find the truth and save
Mrs. Third Floor from being scammed by professional ghost hunters.

Identifiers: LCCN 2020044415 | ISBN 9781534479913 (hardcover) | ISBN 9781534479937 (ebook)

Subjects: CYAC: Ghosts—Fiction. | Pets—Fiction. | Apartment buildings—Fiction. | Swindlers
and swindling—Fiction. | Mystery and detective stories. | Humorous stories.

Classification: LCC PZ7.E21285 Gq 2020 | DDC [Fic]—dc23

LC record available at https://lccn.loc.gov/2020044415

To Cupcake, Pepper, and the dogs of Belmont Park

—E. E.

− 1 −

"NOTHING EXCITING EVER HAPPENS TO US!"
Butterbean wailed, flopping over onto her back in the
living room. She'd hoped that saying that would make
something exciting magically happen, but it didn't work.

She'd done her best to make the day fun. She'd
finished chewing her rawhide chew. She'd disem-
boweled her squeaky lamb toy and carefully scattered
its stuffing around the living room. She'd attempted
to tunnel through the living room carpet (unsuccess-
fully). There was nothing left to do. She'd done it all.

"Nothing! Nothing exciting ever happens!" Butterbean wailed again, in a different key this time. She
liked to mix things up.

Walt rolled her eyes and inspected her paw. "Hello, remember heisting?"

"I wouldn't call an International Crime Syndicate nothing," Oscar sniffed, puffing out his feathers indignantly. He wasn't about to let Butterbean diminish his status as an International Crime Boss. Not to mention the fact that he was the only crime boss who was also a mynah bird. It was no small feat.

Butterbean rolled over onto her stomach. "That was a million years ago. Nothing happens NOW. Just look! Everything's BORING. And even Madison is gone!" Madison was the medium-sized girl who had moved in with them temporarily while her aunt was deployed overseas.

"Madison is at school," Oscar said, absentmindedly flipping through one of Mrs. Food's magazines. "She goes to school every day, Butterbean. It's a thing humans do."

"Not the other day," Butterbean whined. "It wasn't school the other day."

Walt sighed. "We've gone over this, Bean. That was a field trip, and she came back! She always comes back!" Walt shook her head. "You need to get a grip."

"A FIELD TRIP." Butterbean pouted. "WITH-OUT US."

"Let it go, Butterbean," Oscar said, hopping on the

remote to unmute the Television. "The News is back on. They're about to identify the common household appliance that can make us go bald."

Ever since their heist, Oscar had been obsessed with the News. Butterbean wasn't sure why. It wasn't like the News was even talking about their heist anymore. They were old news. On the other hand, she didn't want to go bald.

Butterbean blew on a piece of squeaky-lamb fluff and groaned.

"I get it, Butterbean," Marco said, climbing out of his cage and plunking down next to her. "Us former criminal types have a hard time adjusting to regular life. It's rough. But at least you see Madison. I barely ever see Wallace anymore."

"SEE? Wallace is GONE," Butterbean said triumphantly, sitting up.

"Shhhh," Oscar hissed, turning the volume up on the Television. "Bald, Butterbean."

Walt finished licking her paw. "Moving into a new apartment isn't gone. Wallace just got his own place."

"It's not like he lived with us anyway," Polo

I'VE MOVED TO THE 5TH FLOOR

WALLACE

said, following Marco's lead and climbing out of their cage. "Wallace is still a wild rat, you know."

Wallace was a former pet rat who lived in the Strathmore Building's seventh-floor vents. But a few weeks ago he'd discovered an empty apartment on the fifth floor. And since nobody seemed to be using it, he'd moved his stuff in and sent out change-of-address notices. (Polo thought that was a little formal, but Wallace seemed very proud.)

"Nothing wrong with a little peace and quiet," Walt said, examining her other paw.

"Personally, I like retirement. It's relaxing! We've got Mrs. Food, and how many rats have an extra bonus person to take care of them? We've got it made!" Marco patted Butterbean on the paw.

"And it's not like nothing exciting will ever happen again," Polo said, patting the other paw. "Something exciting could happen AT ANY TIME!"

"Right! Something could happen right now!" Marco chimed in.

Polo nodded. "Or now!"

Marco tilted his head and waited a second. "Or now!"

Polo grinned. "Right. Or now!"

"Cut it out, you guys," Walt said.

"Or not," Polo said. "Maybe not RIGHT now."

4

Walt sighed. "Bean, we can't expect something exciting to happen just because we're bored."

"AHA! So you're bored too!" Butterbean jumped to her feet. "I knew it!" she barked happily. "You—" But she never finished the sentence. Because that's when the pounding started.

Five heads swiveled to look at the front door. The pounding was so loud that they could almost see it— it felt like the door was bouncing inward with each blow. And with each blow the animals cringed and retreated farther into the room.

"Places, everyone!" Oscar screeched, and the animals scrambled so they wouldn't be caught out of their cages. Oscar had barely gotten his cage door closed before Mrs. Food appeared in the hallway, carefully making her way toward the front door. (She was always extra careful now, ever since she'd slipped in a patch of Butterbean's barf and had to go to the hospital. Nobody wanted that to happen again, especially Butterbean. She still felt guilty.)

"Don't open it!" Butterbean yelped. She could feel the hairs on her back prickling. She didn't want to know what was outside in that hallway. Trying to get in.

But Mrs. Food didn't listen.

Taking a deep breath, Mrs. Food threw the door

open. In one swift motion, the thing in the hallway lunged at Mrs. Food, clutching her and sobbing into her shoulder.

"AAAAHHH!" Polo shrieked, diving underneath the cedar bedding in the corner of the cage.

"URGH!" Mrs. Food braced herself against the doorframe as the thing squeezed her. It was shaking and making weird squeaky hiccuppy noises.

Walt crouched down, flexing her claws. "I'll go for the eyes!" Going for the eyes was Walt's go-to attack method.

"Wait, is that . . ." Butterbean sniffed. The monster attacking Mrs. Food smelled very familiar. And it kind of looked more like a hug-attack than an attack-attack. And what kind of monster made squeaky sobs?

"Wait, who . . ." Oscar craned his neck to get a better look.

Butterbean took one last sniff. "It's Mrs. Third Floor!" she gasped.

"Stand down, Walt." Oscar snapped his beak shut. Mrs. Third Floor was not an enemy.

Walt shot him a look in response, but she stayed in attack position. You could never be too sure.

Mrs. Third Floor was a lady from the building, and up until that moment, Butterbean would've said she knew everything about her. After all, she'd seen her around the building since she was a puppy. (Butterbean, not Mrs. Third Floor.)

Mrs. Third Floor lived on the third floor. She wore sturdy leather shoes. She smelled like furniture polish, arthritis cream, and peppermint. She had a scary folding wheely cart that she sometimes took outside. She always spoke to Mrs. Food and patted Butterbean on the head when she saw her. That was pretty much everything there was to know, as far as Butterbean was concerned. But Mrs. Third Floor wasn't a door pounder. And Butterbean had never ever heard her make squeaky noises like that before. She never would've guessed it was possible. Something was very wrong.

Mrs. Food looked as shocked as Butterbean felt. "What is it? What's happened?" Mrs. Food gasped. (Mrs. Third Floor was squeezing her a little too tightly.)

"It's—" Mrs. Third Floor said in a strangled voice. The entire room waited while she choked back a sob. "It's . . ." she said again. "I've had a shock," she finished apologetically.

Mrs. Food nodded. "Here. Sit." She led Mrs. Third Floor toward the sofa and helped her sit down, brushing bits of lamb fluff off the seat.

Butterbean watched with satisfaction. She'd done a very good job distributing the fluff.

"Do you want to talk about it?" Mrs. Food picked up the remote. "I'm sorry about this noise. I don't know how it got turned up so loud."

"No, keep it on—oh darn, we missed that segment on appliances," Mrs. Third Floor sniffled.

Oscar snapped his beak in irritation. He was going to go bald now, he just knew it.

"Mildred." Mrs. Food looked serious. "I don't want to talk about appliances."

"And I don't think I like that anchorwoman's dress. It's not a flattering color." Mrs. Third Floor kept her eyes locked on the Television.

"Mildred . . ."

"Oh and look! Breaking news!" Mrs. Third Floor turned to Mrs. Food with a tight smile on her face. "It's about that octopus at the zoo. Oh no, Mr. Wiggles is missing. That's terrible!"

Mrs. Food turned the Television off. Mrs. Third Floor sagged.

Oscar fluffed his feathers grouchily. First the bald thing, and now this. He was a big fan of Mr. Wiggles. He liked to keep up with all the Wiggles-related news. He just hoped Mrs. Third Floor had a good excuse for the way she was acting.

Mrs. Food patted Mrs. Third Floor on the shoulder. "Mildred, tell me. It's okay. Whatever it is."

Mrs. Third Floor twisted her hands in her lap. "You'll think I'm being silly."

"I won't think you're being silly," Mrs. Food promised.

"Okay." Mrs. Third Floor took a deep breath. "It's that apartment. It's haunted." She burst out in a new round of sobs.

Walt shrugged. "I think she's being silly."

"Huh." Butterbean sat back on her haunches. That hadn't been what she'd expected. "Haunted?"

"I was going to guess a natural disaster," Oscar said. "Although they probably would've covered that on the News. IF WE'D SEEN IT."

"It's just your basic nervous breakdown," Walt said, getting up and stretching. "Nothing to see here."

Mrs. Food had a strange expression on her face. It didn't look like a haunted apartment was what she'd expected either. "Haunted? You mean *haunted* haunted? As in, um . . . ghosts?"

"WAIT, WHAT?" Butterbean yelped. "GHOSTS?"

"She's losing it, Bean," Walt sighed. "There aren't ghosts."

"Yes, GHOSTS," Mrs. Third Floor wailed. "There are GHOSTS in my beautiful rental unit. What am I going to do?"

Mrs. Food scanned the room, like she was going to find the answer lying around somewhere. Like in a book called *Ghosts: How to Handle Them* or *What to Do If Your Friend Flips Out*. "I'm sure there's a reasonable explanation," she said finally.

"THERE IS NO REASONABLE EXPLANATION," Mrs. Third Floor screeched. Her voice was starting to hurt Butterbean's ears, it was that shrill.

"Okay, so explain," Mrs. Food said. "How do you know you have ghosts?"

Mrs. Third Floor took a deep breath. "You know I've been getting that furnished apartment on five ready for renters? Well, for the past few days, there have been SIGNS. OF SUPERNATURAL ACTIVITY." She sat back against the cushions, crossing her arms as if there was no need for further discussion.

Mrs. Food frowned. "Signs?"

"PARANORMAL SIGNS," Mrs. Third Floor snapped. Her jaw was set.

Walt snorted. "Please. As if."

Mrs. Food nodded slowly. "Right. Supernatural activity. Paranormal signs. Of course. Let me get you some tea." She stood up abruptly and hurried over to the kitchen.

Oscar's eyes narrowed. "Wait, five? Did she say the apartment on five?"

Butterbean knew this one. "She did. She said there are GHOSTS. ON FIVE."

Walt shot Oscar a look. "Oh no," she groaned.

"Yep." Oscar sighed.

"What?" Butterbean looked from Walt to Oscar in confusion. She hated it when they had secrets.

"Oh, I know!" Marco piped up from the rat aquarium. "Isn't that where Wallace lives now?"

Walt made a face. "Exactly."

"WHAT?" Butterbean gasped. "WALLACE IS A GHOST?"

"No, Bean. Wallace isn't a ghost. But it's got to be him. Whatever he's been doing is freaking Mrs. Third Floor out. That's the obvious explanation," Oscar said, shaking his head sadly.

"Right. Okay." Butterbean didn't know why Wallace would do something like that, but Oscar usually was right about things. Especially obvious things.

"I don't know," Polo said, fiddling with the button she wore on a string around her neck. "That doesn't sound like Wallace. He's usually pretty careful."

"I know, Polo, but this time—" Walt started, but she never finished the sentence. Because that's when they heard the screaming.

"WHAT IS HAPPENING?" Butterbean barked in alarm. She'd wanted things to get more exciting, but she hadn't counted on there being so much noise.

The screaming was echoing through the vents, and it was so loud that they were sure that even Mrs. Food must hear it.

Five heads swiveled toward the secret vent opening behind the sofa. A few seconds later a small rat came streaking out into the room.

Wallace's eyes were huge. As soon as he saw Walt, he shot over and grabbed her by the leg. "Help! Oh Walt, guys, help!" Wallace gasped.

Butterbean frowned. Polo was right. Wallace was usually a very careful rat. And right now he was being anything but careful.

Walt patted Wallace on the head as she turned her body slightly to hide him from view. Whatever was wrong, it had to be bad if he'd turned to a cat for help. And if he wasn't worried about being seen by the humans, it had to be even worse. "What is it, Wallace?" she said softly.

Wallace looked up at her and took a deep shuddering breath. "It's my apartment! On five! Guys, that apartment is HAUNTED."

– 2 –

"I KNEW IT! WE'VE GOT GHOSTS!" BUTTERBEAN yelped.

"Okay, so maybe it wasn't Wallace," Walt said, frowning.

"Hmm," Oscar said, eyeing Wallace carefully. He'd never seen him so upset. "I have to admit, this is a bit concerning."

"Wallace is definitely more credible than HER," Walt said, jerking her head in the direction of the couch. "But still—ghosts?"

Mrs. Third Floor had taken a tissue out of her pocket and was absentmindedly shredding it. Butterbean watched in approval. She did good work.

"Wallace, we'll need a report." Oscar looked around carefully. Mrs. Third Floor wouldn't be a problem. She wasn't paying attention to anything—she was just staring straight ahead, shredding. But Mrs. Food seemed to be taking a very long time with the tea. She could come back any minute. "Bean, do a Mrs. Food check, please?"

"Gotcha." Butterbean hopped to her feet and did a jaunty walk into the kitchen. A second later she jaunty-walked back into the living room. Mrs. Third Floor didn't even seem to notice. "Mrs. Food is staring at the counter, stirring a cup. She looks like she's in a trance."

Oscar nodded thoughtfully. "Probably trying to buy time." Oscar had a feeling Mrs. Food didn't know how to handle a ghost situation either. "I think we've got a few minutes. Quick, everyone, huddle near the rat cage. Rats, you'll have to stay inside, I'm afraid."

"That's okay," Marco said. "We can hear you. WE'RE HERE FOR YOU, WALLACE!" he shrieked.

"WE'LL TAKE CARE OF THOSE GHOSTS, WALLACE!" Polo smacked her fist into her other hand in a way that would make ghosts tremble.

Walt pushed Wallace into the center of the huddle. "Right. So what *did* you see, exactly?" she asked, keeping an eye on the kitchen as she talked. "Mrs. Third Floor said supernatural activity."

"Oh yes, definitely supernatural. It was terrible. It was just . . . noises, at first. Weird, eerie noises. I thought it was only apartment sounds, but they were everywhere. I could even hear it in the vents. But then I started noticing things . . . moving."

"Moving?" Butterbean shuddered. That didn't sound good. Although, to be fair, she did move quite a bit herself. "You could see them move?"

"No, but things would be different. I left a bunch of sunflower seeds on the table, right? And then when I came back, they'd MOVED. They were scattered all over the floor. And another time, I made a little nest for myself in the fruit bowl, and when I came back from getting dinner, IT WAS GONE. NO FRUIT."

Oscar snapped his beak. "But maybe someone—"

"NO." Wallace shook his head. "There was NO ONE THERE."

Walt frowned. "Could it have been Mrs. Third Floor?"

Wallace shook his head again. "I checked the trash. No fruit peelings or apple cores or anything. The fruit was just gone. ALL OF IT."

"Well, that's strange, but . . ."

Wallace's whiskers trembled. "That's not all. There's

so much more. Like just yesterday, I was in the kitchen, and a salt shaker fell off of the counter and landed right next to me! For no reason. I could've been killed! And I keep thinking—next time, it could be a knife! Or a salt shaker with better aim! Or a piano! I've seen that happen in cartoons a LOT."

"Well, maybe it was a . . ." Oscar trailed off. He couldn't think of what it could've been. Salt shakers didn't usually just jump off of counters. And Wallace was right about pianos. He'd seen it on the Television himself.

"And then today, I was—"

"SHH!" Walt cut him off. "Mrs. Food's coming." Walt threw herself onto the floor in a lounging position to block Wallace, while Oscar flew back into his cage. Butterbean tried a variety of poses, but none of them felt right, so she ended up flopped on her tummy with her tongue lolling out of her mouth.

Their poses didn't matter in the end, though. Mrs. Food didn't even look at them as she walked back into the room carrying a tea tray.

She set the tray down on the coffee table and handed a mug of tea to Mrs. Third Floor. "Mildred," she said slowly. "I don't know what you saw, but we'll get to the bottom of it. I promise."

"But I told you—"

Mrs. Food held up her hand. "I know you think it's ghosts, but it could be something else. We'll do some investigating."

"OOOOH! Investigating! Can we be investigators?" Butterbean hopped to her feet and looked at Walt with her best puppy dog eyes. "If we can't do crimes anymore, we can be ghost investigators. Please?"

"GHOST HUNTERS! YEAH!" Marco cheered.

"YEAH!" Polo echoed.

Walt and Oscar exchanged a glance. "I don't know how much we could do," Walt said. "If Mrs. Food gets involved, it'll be hard. It's not like she'll take us along with her."

Butterbean narrowed her eyes. "Or will she?"

Oscar cocked his head. "Probably not, Bean."

Butterbean slumped. "Yeah, I know. But maybe. OR WE CAN BE SECRET INVESTIGATORS! BEHIND THE SCENES."

"I really appreciate this, guys," Wallace sniffled. "I really liked having an apartment. I was going to invite you over for a sleepover and everything." His chin started to quiver.

Walt patted Wallace on the head, her whiskers trembling. She'd never been on a sleepover.

Mrs. Food cleared her throat. "Now, first things first. As soon as Madison gets back, we'll take a look at this haunted apartment, and then we'll figure this all out." She patted Mrs. Third Floor briskly on the shoulder.

"Thank you, Beulah." Mrs. Third Floor gave Mrs. Food a watery smile. Mrs. Food smiled back brightly. But when she turned away, Mrs. Food's smile disappeared completely.

"Got that, guys?" Walt looked up at the clock. "Madison will be back any minute. When they leave, we can check in with Chad. He might have heard something about ghosts."

Chad was the last member of their heisting gang, known by his nickname "the Octopus." (A nickname he'd gotten because he was, in fact, an octopus.)

"Good plan," Oscar agreed. "And while you do that, I can hold down the fort here." He eyed the clock. If Madison got home soon, he might be able to catch the second half of the News.

The waiting was agony.

Walt watched the door. Marco and Polo shot encouraging looks and thumbs-ups to Wallace. Mrs. Food and Mrs. Third Floor sipped tea and nibbled awkwardly on cookies. Butterbean focused on looking cute and watching for stray cookie crumbs. (She kind of forgot about the whole ghost thing once the cookies came out.) And Oscar watched the clock. He was going to miss the rest of the News. He just knew it.

They were so focused on waiting that it came as a shock when Madison finally burst into the room.

"Mrs. Fudeker! Did you hear about Mr. Wiggles? He's disappeared!" She dumped her book bag on the floor next to the front door and then checked the kitchen quickly before rushing into the living room. "I saw him during my field trip the other day. I bet I was one of the last people to see him before he—"

She stopped short when she saw Mrs. Third Floor on the couch, sniffling.

"Oh. Um. Hi, Mrs. . . ."

"Third Floor," Butterbean barked. "Mrs. Third Floor."

"Mildred, you know Madison. She's Ruby Park's niece. She's living here temporarily, and I thought she might like to go up with us to check out the . . . um . . . activity in your apartment."

"Yes, that would be nice," Mrs. Third Floor said bleakly. She sounded like she'd given up all hope.

Madison shifted from one foot to the other. "Sure. So, what kind of activity?"

"Paranormal," Mrs. Third Floor sniffled.

"Mildred thinks she has a ghost," Mrs. Food said matter-of-factly. She didn't meet Madison's eyes.

"Oh, wow." Madison's eyebrows shot up. "Um, okay. I can help," she said, nodding slowly. "Ghosts stink."

"We'll just take a look, real quick." Mrs. Food nodded. "Just to see what there is to see."

"Um. Okay," Madison said. "I'm up for it, I guess." Ghosts sounded weird, but she'd been in some pretty weird situations before. She glanced over at the rat aquarium. There were some things she didn't even try to understand.

Butterbean dragged her eyes away from the cookies and hurried over to Madison. "I've got to try," she muttered to Oscar as she went. "We could be an International Investigator Syndicate! Famous detectives!"

Butterbean leaned hard against Madison's leg and looked up significantly. She really wished Madison had learned to speak Dog.

When Madison looked down, Butterbean shot another significant look at the door and then looked back up at Madison expectantly. It was the best she could do.

"Sorry, Butterbean, I'll take you out afterward," Madison said, patting Butterbean on the head. Butterbean wuffled in frustration.

"NO!" Mrs. Third Floor snapped. She jumped up and pointed at Butterbean like she'd seen a snake. Butterbean was a little offended, to be honest. "Take her, too!"

"What?" Madison jerked up in surprise.

"Take the dog. And the cat. All the animals. The

bird? Maybe not the bird. But maybe?" She leaned over to Mrs. Food. "I've heard that animals are very sensitive to THE OTHER SIDE."

Mrs. Food took a deep breath. "Sure. Take the animals. Why not?" She had not expected her day to go quite this way, but she might as well go all in.

Then she hesitated. "But you're right, maybe not the bird. Just the dog and cat." She shot Oscar an apologetic look. He tried not to feel offended. Taking his cage along would've been impractical, he could see that. They didn't realize that he was perfectly capable of flying himself.

"Madison, get Butterbean's leash. And, I don't know, carry Walt, I guess. We're going up to five to check things out."

"Ookay." Madison squinted at Mrs. Food like she was hoping an explanation would be on Mrs. Food's face. But there was nothing—the only sign that something was up was a slight twitch near Mrs. Food's left eye. Madison turned and went to get Butterbean's leash.

Butterbean did a happy little dance. "It worked!"

"So, new plan," Walt said dryly. "Got it."

Butterbean danced over to the edge of the sofa where Wallace was hiding. "Wallace, climb on," she said under her breath as she danced past.

"Really?" Wallace said uncertainly. "I don't know. . . ."

"You need to show us what you saw, right? I got us in on Mrs. Food's investigation! Hurry!" Butterbean could only dance for so long.

Wallace clenched his fists. "Right. You're right." As Butterbean did another dance-by, he grabbed hold of the fur under her tummy and pulled himself up.

"Okay, this plan works too, I guess," Walt said in a strangled voice as Madison scooped her up by the middle.

"No fair!" Marco squealed.

"I can't believe we have to stay behind!" Polo grumbled as she watched them gather by the door.

"Yes, so unfair," Oscar said, eyeing the remote.

"Hold on tight, Wallace! Butterbean has slippery hair!" Polo yelled as they left.

"Go get 'em, guys! Good luck, Walt!" Marco shouted.

Walt could only nod as she was carried out. No matter what they found upstairs, she knew one thing. There were some things worse than ghosts.

– 3 –

THE DOOR TO APARTMENT 5B LOOKED LIKE any other door in the Strathmore Building, except that it had been recently painted.

"It doesn't look haunted," Butterbean said, examining it. She sniffed it tentatively, but the paint fumes were too strong for her to get a sense of what was inside. Besides, she didn't know what ghosts smelled like.

"Anything, Bean?" Walt asked, dangling from Madison's arms. She would've preferred to ride on her shoulders, but apparently it wasn't her decision.

"Nothing. Just paint. And I don't hear any scary noises, either."

"Interesting." From what Wallace had said, Walt had been expecting rattling chains and horrible wails.

Mrs. Food turned to Mrs. Third Floor, who was still hanging back by the elevator. "Mildred?"

Mrs. Third Floor nodded and walked slowly over to the door, like she was afraid it was going to jump out and bite her. Then she carefully leaned down and unlocked it.

"There! Done." She clenched her hands tightly in front of her. "And I know what you're thinking—I changed the locks after the last tenant moved out. All the keys are accounted for."

"That's not what I was thinking," Butterbean whispered to Wallace.

"That was going to be my first question," Mrs. Food said. "Ready?"

"Ready," Mrs. Third Floor said.

"Ready," Madison said.

"Ready," Wallace said, clinging tightly to Butterbean's tummy hair.

Mrs. Food opened the door.

The door to Apartment 5B creaked ominously as it swung open.

Mrs. Third Floor winced. "I'll have to get maintenance to fix that," she said nervously. With a quick glance at Mrs. Food, she stepped into the apartment.

She'd barely set foot inside before she gasped and jumped back into Madison.

"Whoa!" Madison stumbled back to get out of her way. "You okay?"

Mrs. Third Floor pointed a quivering finger in the direction of the living room.

"There!" she wailed. "Don't you see? The ghost!"

Butterbean scrambled to get inside. Walt turned her bones to jelly and slid down onto the floor, escaping Madison's grip. Then she peered around Mrs. Third Floor's legs to get a better look. But unless the ghost was covered with floral upholstery, he wasn't making himself obvious.

The apartment was a lot like Mrs. Food's apartment, but with much newer and fancier furniture. It looked like something out of a catalog, or a furniture commercial on the Television. It didn't look like someplace a ghost would hang out. It totally looked like someplace Wallace would hang out, though.

Mrs. Food cleared her throat as she looked around. "Um, where is the ghost, exactly?"

Mrs. Third Floor made a strangled sound. "Not the ghost HIMSELF, but you can see he's been here. Look! The remote is sitting in the middle of the couch. IT'S ON THE COUCH! I WOULD NEVER LEAVE IT LIKE THAT."

"I know, I know." Mrs. Food patted Mrs. Third Floor on the shoulder.

"Oh shoot. Yeah, that's me," Wallace said from underneath Butterbean's stomach. "I did that one."

Walt rolled her eyes.

"What can I say, I like my shows." Wallace attempted to shrug, but he only managed to slide down closer to Butterbean's legs.

"Watch it, Wallace," Butterbean grumbled.

"SEE? Even the dog can sense the presence!" Mrs. Third Floor said. She went over to the haunted remote and poked it with one finger. "Do you think it's cursed?"

Mrs. Food walked over carefully and picked up the remote. Mrs. Third Floor gasped. "Don't touch it!"

"It seems fine to me, Mildred." She pointed it at the Television and clicked it on.

It was a home shopping channel. The salespeople onscreen were very excited about a new line of cookware. Butterbean sniffed. She wasn't interested in cookware.

"YOU SEE?" Mrs. Third Floor screeched. "I WOULD NEVER WATCH THAT."

"Home shopping?" Walt said, raising an eyebrow.

"Oh that . . . um. Not me, that's for sure," Wallace stammered. "That . . . um . . . Wow, that's some ghost. Spooky."

Walt shook her head.

"A rat can dream, okay?" Wallace blurted out. "Sheesh."

Mrs. Third Floor grabbed the remote and changed the channel. "See! THAT's where it should be!"

It was the Hallmark Channel. It seemed to be showing some kind of Christmas movie, even though it wasn't anywhere near Christmas.

"Wow, it IS haunted," Butterbean said, examining the twinkling Christmas tree lights on the screen. "The Television doesn't even know what time of year it is!"

"Butterbean," Walt started, but she was cut off by a shriek from Mrs. Third Floor.

"AND THERE!" Mrs. Third Floor pointed a trembling finger at the kitchen island, where an elaborate tiered cupcake display was set up. They were all beautifully frosted, except for the bottom row of cupcakes, which had the frosting almost completely licked off. "THE GHOST RUINED MY CUPCAKES!"

Wallace shifted uncomfortably. "Um, yeah. That would be me again."

Walt let her breath out in a huff. "Wallace, are we sure you're not the ghost?"

"It's not me, I swear! I SAW THINGS."

Mrs. Food inspected one of the licked cupcakes. "It does look strange, but I don't know if it looks paranormal. . . ."

Madison took the cupcake and examined it. Then she shot a suspicious look at Butterbean.

Butterbean gasped. "WHY IS SHE LOOKING AT ME?"

"You do seem like a likely suspect," Walt said smugly. "Even if you are innocent."

"But that's not all." Mrs. Third Floor grabbed Mrs. Food's arm and dragged her away from the cupcakes. "That's just what's new. I haven't even shown you the worst of it. How do you explain THAT?"

She pointed at a large fish tank partly obscured by leafy ferns in the corner of the room. It had obviously been just as fancy as the rest of the apartment at one time, with lots of brightly colored rocks and plants. It even had a little diver and treasure chest in the middle. But the lid to the tank had been shoved to the side and was half submerged in what was left of the water. The rest had been sloshed onto the floor and spread like a stain on the carpet. But that wasn't the worst part. There were no fish.

"Um." Mrs. Food frowned.

"Not me," Wallace squeaked. "I swear, not me at all."

"My beautiful tropical fish display! WHERE ARE

THEY?" Mrs. Third Floor demanded. "They're all GONE."

"That's . . . um . . ." Madison said, examining the tank. Walt sniffed at it too. Her stomach started to growl.

"And look!" Mrs. Third Floor dragged Mrs. Food down the hallway and pushed her into the bathroom. Butterbean and Walt had to scramble to keep up with them.

This time it was Mrs. Food who gasped. "But everything's wet!" She picked up a dripping bath towel and held it carefully away from herself. The bath mat squelched under their feet, and there were pools of water all around it. The tub was half-filled with leftover cloudy water. There were dribbles of water half dried on the walls.

"THOSE WERE DECORATIVE," Mrs. Third Floor wailed, pointing at the hand towels, which lay in a wet pile on the floor. "AND JUST LOOK AT MY TINY SOAPS!"

The remains of tiny soaps that once probably looked like little shells or bows or something fancy lay in a mushy mass in the soap dishes. They were definitely not decorative anymore.

"This is terrible," Mrs. Food said, ushering Mrs. Third Floor out of the bathroom. "But do ghosts usually do this kind of thing?"

"Poltergeists do, right?" Madison said softly. She shivered, looking around like a poltergeist was going to creep up behind her. "Aren't poltergeists the kind of ghosts that break things?"

"Yes!" Mrs. Third Floor said triumphantly. "Poltergeists! I have a poltergeist!"

"That may be true, but I'm still not convinced," Mrs. Food said. "Why don't you sit while Madison and I look around."

"Mrs. Food may be right," Butterbean said, sniffing the soggy towel. "I'm not getting a ghost feeling."

"Do you know what a ghost feeling is?" Wallace asked.

"No," Butterbean admitted.

Mrs. Food helped Mrs. Third Floor over to the sofa and then went through the apartment room by room. Butterbean stood in the middle of the living room, head up to catch any stray smells. She wasn't sure where she was supposed to look for ghosts.

"That fish tank's what did it for me. It scared the heck out of me." Wallace's voice floated up from her tummy area. "Water was everywhere. I was in the kitchen when it happened. Water exploded out of the tank, and I ran."

"How did you even get in here, Wallace?" Walt asked. "You can't fit through the vent cover."

Wallace blew a piece of Butterbean's hair out of his mouth before answering. "There's a behind-the-sofa vent here, too. I used that. I got the screws out with a piece of metal from the loading dock."

"Smart," Walt said. "And nobody else has used it?"

"No, definitely not. I put a whisker over the entrance to see if anyone else came in. It was always still there when I came back."

"Hmm." Walt looked around the room again, deep in thought.

Mrs. Food and Madison finished their inspections

and came back to Mrs. Third Floor, who was staring blankly at a gingerbread house competition on the Television.

"Well, I didn't find anything. I can't see how this happened," Mrs. Food said, wiping her hands on her pants.

"Poltergeist," Mrs. Third Floor said. "Like Madison said."

Madison folded her arms in front of her chest. "Maybe? But maybe not." She frowned at the licked cupcakes. "This is creepy, but I'm not sure it's ghost creepy. In any case . . ." She looked at Mrs. Food.

Mrs. Food put her hand on Mrs. Third Floor's shoulder. "Whatever happened here is a crime. We need to call the police."

− 4 −

IT DIDN'T TAKE THE POLICE LONG TO GET there. And it took even less time for them to realize that their biggest problem was Mrs. Third Floor herself.

"I don't know why you're here," she grumbled as she let the two police officers in. "I don't see what the police can do about a ghost."

"Poltergeist," Madison corrected helpfully.

"RIGHT. Poltergeist," Mrs. Third Floor agreed, crossing her arms. "But since you're here, go ahead, take a look. The apartment has been DESTROYED. By SUPERNATURAL FORCES."

"Or by an intruder," Mrs. Food said apologetically.

"We're thinking it's probably just an intruder, Officer . . ."

"Marlowe." The first police officer introduced herself, giving Mrs. Third Floor an appraising look. "And this is Officer Travis." Officer Travis nodded. He looked almost as grumpy as Mrs. Third Floor.

Officer Marlowe took out a notebook. "Why don't you show me what we've got here?"

"Well—" Mrs. Food started.

"EVIL SPIRITS," Mrs. Third Floor interrupted, waving her arms to indicate invisible spirits, "ATE MY CUPCAKES."

"Just the frosting," Wallace muttered under his breath.

Mrs. Food took a step forward, smiling tightly. "As I said, there was an intruder. They destroyed a fish tank, vandalized the bathroom, and ate food in the kitchen. We just don't know how they got in."

"This may be an unearthly portal." Mrs. Third Floor's mouth was set in a grim line. "Maybe in the bathroom?" she added thoughtfully. "I don't even know how you list an unearthly portal," she said to herself.

"So . . . intruder. Got it." Officer Marlowe wrote it down in her notebook. "And this is your apartment?" she asked Mrs. Third Floor.

"Oh, heavens no. I mean, yes, of course. I mean, not

really," Mrs. Third Floor said. Officer Travis sighed and folded his arms in front of his chest.

Mrs. Third Floor cleared her throat. Her ears were turning red. "It's a rental unit. I'm the landlady. I'm getting it ready to rent. My old tenant moved to Tulsa."

"Man Who Smells Like Onions," Butterbean whispered knowingly to Walt and Wallace. "I did

NOT like sharing an elevator with him, let me tell you."

"I see." Officer Marlowe gave the apartment an appraising look. "And this is what, one, two bedrooms?"

"Two bedrooms. But I have it set up as a bedroom and an office."

"Interesting." Officer Marlowe flipped a page in her pad and made a note. "One thousand square feet, I'm guessing?"

"Eleven hundred," Mrs. Third Floor answered.

"Aha." Officer Marlowe made another note. Officer Travis shot her a look. "So not a lot of room to hide, is what I'm saying," she said, glaring back at Officer Travis. Then she smiled at Mrs. Food. "Now, you said someone ate the food in the kitchen?"

"Yes, see!" Mrs. Third Floor pointed to the cupcakes. "See? The frosting there is all gone. Some . . . THING . . . pierced the thin veil separating the living from the dead and . . . well . . ."

"Licked the cupcakes?" Officer Travis said, picking one up and examining it.

"Well. Yes." Mrs. Third Floor shifted. "As you can see."

"Or," Mrs. Food jumped in, "another theory is that a person did it. That's why we called you."

"Or," Walt said quietly, "a rat did it."

"Ooh, I'll go with that one," Butterbean said.

"You guys," Wallace groaned. "Stop it. There really is a ghost."

"And you, little girl. You don't know anything about these?" Officer Travis said, waving the licked cupcake in Madison's direction. "Pretty tempting, aren't they?"

"I guess?" Madison looked confused. "They were licked when I got here, though, so not really?" She didn't know anyone who thought licked cupcakes were tempting. Except maybe Officer Travis.

"Right." Officer Travis narrowed his eyes at her and put the cupcake down.

Officer Marlowe ran her finger along the countertop and examined it. "And this countertop. Is this . . . granite?"

"What? Yes," Mrs. Third Floor. "Do you think that has something to do with it?"

"It's possible," Officer Marlowe said.

"But probably not," Officer Travis said, frowning at Officer Marlowe. "What we need to do is evaluate the scene. Now, the bedroom is through that door?"

Mrs. Third Floor nodded. "Right. And the bathroom was totally destroyed—it's right through there. There's water everywhere."

Officer Marlowe made a note. "I'll take a look." Then she hesitated. "Is that the only bathroom?"

"Yes, it is," Mrs. Third Floor said.

Officer Marlowe frowned. "I see." She turned and headed down the hall.

Officer Travis clapped his hands together loudly. They all jumped. Wallace almost lost his grip on Butterbean completely. "Ladies," he said in a booming voice. "Please take the kids and livestock and remain in the living room area for the duration of our search." He glared down at Mrs. Food. "We don't want them destroying evidence, got it?"

"Got it," Mrs. Food said. She turned to Madison. "Okay, KIDS. You heard him."

"How many people does he think I am?" Madison whispered, sitting down on the couch. "Sheesh!"

"LIVESTOCK?" Butterbean huffed. "I've never been so offended."

"That makes two of us. If he wasn't wearing a uniform, I'd go for the jugular." Walt jumped up onto the couch and settled in a pounce stance.

"That makes three of us," Wallace said. "And I don't even think he knows about me."

"Maybe he thinks you're one of the kids," Butterbean said.

"Hush, dog," Madison said, rubbing Butterbean's ear. "This is important. Do you sense any ghosts?"

Butterbean thumped her tail. She figured Madison could interpret that anyway she wanted to.

"I didn't think so," Madison said, her eyes narrowed.

Butterbean made a mental note that thumping meant no.

"If I'm right, the animals are protecting us from the forces of evil," Mrs. Third Floor said, wringing her hands nervously.

"Sure," Madison said, shooting a look at Mrs. Food.

Mrs. Food clamped her lips together tightly and stared at the ceiling.

Butterbean stood a little taller. She'd never protected anyone from the forces of evil before.

"Oh brother," Walt sighed.

"I get why Mrs. Food called the police," Butterbean said after a few minutes of waiting. "But how are we supposed to do any investigating if we're sitting on the couch?"

"We're not," Walt said, stalking along the back of the sofa. "We need a new plan."

"What are we going to do?" Wallace shifted.

"Leave it to me," Walt said. "But for now, we watch. And wait."

"So, what, we're just supposed to WAIT until they get back?" Marco wailed from the top of the water bottle.

"Shhh! I can't hear!" Oscar had turned the Television back on and was watching the News. He had the volume turned down low, so he'd be able to hear Mrs. Food's key and get back to his cage in time. That was the theory, anyway.

"But anything could've happened! They could've all been eaten by GHOSTS," Marco said.

"It's true! We'd never know!" Polo chimed in. "We need to do something."

"We need to stay here," Oscar said, keeping one eye on the Television. They were just about to give tips on decorating your small space. And Oscar didn't know anyone who had a smaller space than him. (Well, maybe the rats, but they didn't do much in the way of decorating.) His cage could really use a few pops of color.

"Harrumph." Marco threw himself into a pile of cedar chips.

"You said it," Polo said. "Harrumph."

As she spoke, a cabinet door slammed in the kitchen. The rats froze. Oscar cranked the volume on the Television another notch higher.

"Ghosts?" Marco whispered to Polo, still not daring to move.

"Maybe?" Polo whispered back. "Or maybe it's just—"

The electric can opener started whirring.

"CHAD," Polo finished, flopping over backward in relief.

"HI, CHAD!" Marco waved. He nudged Polo in the side. "Maybe we can do some investigating of our own!"

He scrambled out of the cage and scurried to the kitchen. "HEY, CHAD! We've got a very important question for you!"

"YES!" Polo hurried after him. "Very important!"

Chad the octopus was sitting in the sink eating a can of salmon. He hardly looked up when they came in.

Marco skidded to a stop and watched Chad eat. It really was something to see. "Um, Chad. So we have something really important to ask you." Marco hesitated.

Chad kept eating. "So you said. Three times."

"Right. So . . ." Marco tried to figure out what to say. Now that he was standing there, asking about ghosts felt a little . . . well, dumb.

"It's, um . . ." Polo hesitated too. She and Marco exchanged glances.

"Ghosts," Marco blurted out. It sounded even sillier now that he'd actually said it. "Have you seen any ghosts?"

Chad stopped eating. A little bit of salmon fell out of his mouth. "What?"

"Ghosts," Polo said. "You know. Spirits? Apparitions? Like oooOOOOOOOooooooooOOOOO . . ." Polo made scary ghost noises and waved her arms in a ghostly way.

"Um. Yeah. Like that." Marco cringed, grabbing Polo's arm and dragging it down to her side. "Ghosts. We heard there were ghosts on the fifth floor."

"Have you heard that?" Polo asked, smoothing her fur down self-consciously.

"Ghosts?" Chad stared at them. "On the fifth floor?"

"Yeah," Polo said, cringing inwardly.

Chad made a snorty sound. "In a word, no. No ghosts, not on five, or anywhere else. That's ridiculous." He turned back to his salmon. "Was that all?"

Marco blushed. "Um, well . . ." He couldn't think of any way to turn the conversation around to make it less awkward. He shot a desperate look at Polo.

"I like what you're doing with your . . . uh . . . tentacles," Polo blurted out. "It's a good look." She really wished she hadn't made the ghost noises.

Chad's eyes narrowed. "What about my tentacles?" He finished his salmon and flipped the can in the air so that it landed in the trash can across the room. He was a very good shot.

"Nothing," Marco said, grabbing Polo's arm. "It's not important. That's all, Chad. See you later."

He dragged Polo back into the living room. "It's a good look?" he whispered.

Polo made a face. "I know! I couldn't think what to say. But you know what we've got?"

Marco frowned. "What?"

"We've got exclusive information. Walt is going to be so surprised!" Polo said smugly, holding up her hand. "HIGH FIVE!"

Marco smacked her hand. The ghost hunters were on the case.

"I don't think they're even looking for a ghost," Butterbean said, watching Officer Travis sniff a lemon that had been set out in a decorative tray. "He touched that with his nose."

"I'm not eating that one," Wallace said, shuddering slightly. "The ghost can have it."

"I don't think we're going to get any answers this way," Walt said, watching Officer Travis put the lemon back and then scratch his armpit.

"Me either," Butterbean said. "Unless . . . DO YOU THINK THAT LEMON IS HAUNTED?"

"Get real, Butterbean. It's a lemon," Wallace

grumbled. "What he needs to be looking at is that salt shaker. It tried to kill me!"

Walt attempted to pat Wallace on the back, but it wasn't easy with Wallace hanging under Butterbean's stomach. She just ended up whacking Butterbean in the leg. Madison gave her a strange look.

Officer Marlowe came out of the bathroom and headed over to Mrs. Third Floor.

"I think we've got all we need here. I made a note of the water in your bathroom. That was quite a mess."

Mrs. Third Floor gave her a teary smile. "Thank you."

Officer Marlowe nodded. "I just have one last question. Now, that water, is that included in the rent?"

"Well, yes." Mrs. Third Floor blinked. "Water, gas, electric—I include all utilities."

Officer Marlowe raised her eyebrows. "Really. That's VERY interesting." She made another note on her notepad before putting it back in her pocket. "We'll be in touch. In the meantime, you might want to get some sort of surveillance camera for the front door." She turned to leave, and then hesitated. "And, as a precaution, I don't think you should rent the unit until we've gotten to the bottom of this."

"Of course." Mrs. Third Floor nodded. "I'll get a camera installed first thing in the morning. But you know that ghosts don't appear on camera."

Officer Marlowe kept her face blank. "Right. We'll see ourselves out."

The two officers exchanged a glance as they headed for the door.

Mrs. Third Floor gave a small hiccuppy sob.

Mrs. Food hurried over and rubbed her arm. "It'll be okay, Mildred. We'll get this sorted out." She turned back to Madison. "Ready?"

Madison stood up. "Let's go, guys."

Walt leaned over. "Wallace, do you want to stay here? You could just go back to your vent."

Wallace shook his head, making it look like Butterbean was trying to do the hula. "I'd rather stay close to Butterbean here. It makes me feel safer."

"That's fine," Walt said. "And it doesn't matter. We'll be back soon enough."

"We will?" Butterbean said.

"If we're going to investigate, we have to move fast, before those cameras are in place. It'll have to be tonight."

"Wait, you mean . . ." Wallace said softly.

"Yes." Walt stood up and unsheathed the claws on her left paw. "That means one thing. We're having a sleepover."

– 5 –

OSCAR HAD TO ADMIT, HE WAS LOOKING forward to doing some serious investigating. He just wished Walt had called it what it was—a stakeout. Because the word "sleepover" was having an unfortunate effect on the other animals.

"WHY DON'T I HAVE PAJAMAS!" Marco wailed. "How am I supposed to have a sleepover without pajamas!"

"SHHH!" Walt hissed at him. She glanced nervously at the dining room, where Madison and Mrs. Food were having dinner. Fortunately, they didn't seem to have noticed the ruckus. To be fair, it had been a pretty exhausting day. Mrs. Third Floor hadn't left for ages. "Keep it down!" Walt hissed. "Stop attracting attention. Do you want them to find Wallace?"

Wallace had decided to hide out in Marco and Polo's aquarium until it was time for the sleepover. So far Mrs. Food hadn't noticed the extra rat in their cage. (They'd been very carefully flopping into a heap whenever she walked by. It wasn't easy to tell how many rats there were when they were in a heap. Unless you counted tails, which luckily, Mrs. Food didn't usually do.)

"FINE. I'LL GO NAKED. I just feel so unprepared," Marco sighed. "No pajamas, no fuzzy slippers, no popcorn, nothing. Do we even have movies to watch?"

"WE DON'T EVEN HAVE SLEEPING BAGS!" Polo wailed.

"There might be popcorn, actually!" Wallace said, sticking his head out from under a pile of cedar chips. "I think Mrs. Third Floor had some in the cabinet. She said something about making the apartment smell homey. I bet she wouldn't mind if we ate it."

"Well, at least we'll have something," Marco said. He could always go for a good piece of popcorn.

"And there are probably movies on TV!" Wallace said. "And if there aren't, there's always the home shopping channel. I think tonight's the Cubic Zirconia Extravaganza!"

"OOH, SPARKLY," Polo sighed. She had her sparkly button, sure, but she always had room for more sparkly things in her life.

"Remember, this is supposed to be a stakeout, not a party," Oscar said. "We're staking out the ghost."

Butterbean wrinkled her nose. "Yeah, but Walt didn't say stakeout. She said sleepover. And I don't have pajamas either."

"Well, you don't need pajamas for a stakeout," Oscar huffed, puffing out his feathers. He just hoped that if they really did find the ghost, they'd be able to handle it. Ghosts were serious business.

Walt sat down next to the rat cage. "Look, I can't do pajamas, but I think I can get you guys sleeping bags. Okay?"

"Oh, Walt, that would be awesome!" Polo cheered. This was shaping up to be the best sleepover ever. As long as she didn't think about the ghost part, that is.

"Okay, so here's the plan. We wait until everyone's gone to bed. Butterbean obviously can't go through the vents, so I thought I'd go with her in the hallway. Oscar, you and the rats open the door for us when we get there."

"Wait, how are we getting there?" Polo asked, tilting her head to the side.

Walt shrugged. "The vents. Obviously."

"Oh no. I'm sorry, but no. I'll go on Butterbean's

tummy, thank you. I don't want to be in those vents alone." Wallace crossed his arms defiantly.

"HEY!" Polo said indignantly. "What am I, chopped liver?"

"YOU KNOW WHAT I MEAN!" Wallace glared at her. "IT'S NOT SAFE."

"But you love the vents!" Oscar said. "They're your home!"

Wallace shook his head. "Nope. Not until that ghost is gone, they aren't. I'll stick with Walt and Butterbean." He shot Polo a look. "WALT'S BIG."

Walt sighed. "Fine. Oscar, you and Marco and Polo can handle the door."

"Um. I think I'd rather go with Wallace, okay?" Polo toed the floor of the cage nervously.

"Yeah. Me too," Marco said. "Safety in numbers, right?"

Walt groaned. "The more of us there are in the hallway, the more risky it is!" She couldn't believe the others were being so silly. "Fine, Oscar, we'll meet you there."

Oscar shot a sideways glance at Walt and cleared his throat. "Um."

"NOT YOU TOO!" Walt burst out. "We are supposed to be INVESTIGATORS. How are we supposed to investigate if we're a bunch of chickens!"

"Sorry," Marco said.

"Bawk bawk," Polo said softly.

"Walt, you haven't seen the classic horror movies on the Television. You don't know what happens when the Television people split up." Oscar shuddered. "It's not pretty."

Walt groaned. "So all of us are just going to traipse through the hallways and hope nobody sees us? Is that really our plan?"

Butterbean patted Walt on the shoulder. "Trust me. It'll be fine."

It took forever for Madison and Mrs. Food to get ready for bed. Butterbean had a feeling they were spooked by all the ghost talk too. They'd never left the bathroom light on all night before.

Finally, Oscar opened the door to his cage and hopped out. "Bean! Help me check!"

Oscar flew down the hallway and hovered outside Mrs. Food's door. "Nothing."

Butterbean nosed at the bottom of the door and cocked her head. "Snoring. We're good."

Oscar flew to Madison's door and did the same check. "Sounds good. Bean?"

Butterbean nodded. "Asleep."

Oscar flew back into the living room. "All clear. Everybody ready? Let's go."

Walt didn't move. She just sat in the living room and twitched her tail back and forth. "And how exactly are we going to get inside?" She was still irritated about the whole vent thing.

Oscar held out a claw with a flourish. In it was a shiny silver key. "Voilà!"

Walt's eyes got wide. "Where did you get that?"

"Mrs. Food's pocket. Mrs. Third Floor gave it to her before she left," Oscar said smugly. "I thought we could, you know, borrow it. Just for a little while."

"Well done," Walt said grudgingly. "But I still think this is a ridiculous plan."

"It'll be fine!" Marco said, walking over to her. He was carrying a tissue bundle filled with sunflower seeds. He patted it lovingly. "Snacks. Now should I just climb up or . . ."

Walt rolled her eyes. "FINE. Just one second." Walt

disappeared behind the couch and reappeared a few minutes later with a small bag hanging around her neck. Then she lay down. "Hop up," she said. Marco and Polo quickly scrambled onto her back.

Oscar eyed the bag. "That's one of Mrs. Food's."

"Like you said. I'm borrowing it," Walt said, standing up. "Polo, can you be in charge of the key?"

Polo nodded solemnly as Oscar handed her the key. "I'll guard it with my life."

Walt looked uncomfortable. "Erm, okay?" She really didn't think it would come to that.

Butterbean nosed Wallace. "You coming with me?"

"Sure," Wallace said. He grabbed on to Butterbean's hair and held on under her tummy. He didn't think he'd be comfortable being exposed like Marco and Polo were. He'd been a wild rat too long now.

Oscar flew over to the countertop and picked up a bright orange flyer from the local pizza place. Then he flew over to the front door and pushed down on the handle with his feet. It swung open just enough for Walt and Butterbean to squeeze through.

Walt and Butterbean held the door open while Oscar flew through the crack. Then, as he slipped the flyer in between the door and the latch, they let it close. "It can't lock if that flyer's in there," Oscar explained. "We can get back in this way."

"You've obviously been thinking about this," Walt said approvingly. "Nice trick."

"Save the congratulations until we see if it works," Oscar said, looking around the hallway nervously. "Maybe the vents would have been better."

"Too late now," Walt said. "Of course, somebody could see that piece of paper. It's pretty obvious."

Oscar cringed. He should've gone for something in a nice white or beige. But it was too late to worry about that now. Besides, the paper was the least of their concerns. He didn't think anyone would be up at this time of night, but if someone did see them, their whole plan would fall apart. He didn't know how they would explain being in the hallway. Oscar puffed up his feathers and sniffed. "Not a problem. We'll be back before that happens." He just hoped it was true.

Walt stalked over to the elevator. "Butterbean, would you do the honors?"

"Oh boy!" Butterbean squealed, jumping up and pressing the elevator button with her nose. She was an expert at elevator button pushing.

Oscar flew over and landed on her head, his feet clutching tightly to her ears. He'd never been in an elevator without his cage before. He didn't know what to expect.

"Remember, we don't go until it's empty," Walt said, her whiskers twitching nervously. This whole plan was wrong. They were too exposed. The last thing they needed was for Butterbean to be reckless.

Butterbean rolled her eyes. "It's the middle of the night! Who would be in the elevator in the middle of the night?"

The elevator bell sounded. The doors opened.

It wasn't empty.

An elderly woman wearing a housedress was standing in the elevator, holding a laundry basket. Mrs. Power Walker.

"Perfect!" Butterbean barked. "Hi, Mrs. Power Walker!"

"Butterbean, no!" Walt started, but it was too late. Butterbean didn't hesitate. With Oscar still clinging tightly to the top of her head, Butterbean marched into the elevator, pressed the button for five, and sat down. She wagged her tail at Mrs. Power Walker.

Walt cursed slightly under her breath. Mrs. Power Walker had been pretty accepting of Walt and Butterbean in the past, but there was no way she was going to be able to overlook three rats and a bird. The last thing Walt wanted was Marco and Polo waving their arms and screaming like they were on a roller coaster.

"Not a word," she hissed at the rats. She darted

into the elevator and sat down just as the doors closed.

The rats didn't need to be told. As soon as they'd seen Mrs. Power Walker, Marco and Polo had flattened themselves to Walt's back in their best attempt to turn invisible. It didn't work.

Mrs. Power Walker smiled at Butterbean sympathetically. "Couldn't sleep?"

Butterbean thumped her tail and lolled her tongue out of her mouth.

Mrs. Power Walker winked. "I couldn't either. Thought I'd get a little laundry done since I was up." She nodded toward her laundry basket.

Oscar fidgeted in place and stared straight ahead. He didn't know if he was supposed to say anything back. He wasn't up on his elevator etiquette.

"A nice walk before bed will be just the thing for you," Mrs. Power Walker said. Then she frowned, seeming to notice Oscar and the rats for the first time. "And your . . . friends."

Oscar attempted a smile, but his beak wasn't really made that way.

Marco and Polo blinked up at her, their eyes huge. Mrs. Power Walker blinked back.

"Fifth floor," the elevator voice said. The doors opened.

Butterbean wagged her tail at Mrs. Power Walker and then trotted out, with Walt slinking behind her like a shadow. Mrs. Power Walker looked at them thoughtfully as the doors closed.

"Holy cow, that was CRAZY!" Marco's eyes were huge. "Did you see? She looked RIGHT AT US! And she didn't say a THING!"

"Mrs. Power Walker's nice," Butterbean said. "Not like Mrs. Hates Dogs on six."

Oscar closed his eyes. He was never great in social

situations. He'd learned his lesson. He should've definitely gone with the vents, haunted or not.

"Never mind Mrs. Power Walker," he said, hopping off Butterbean's head. "We're here."

They turned to look at Apartment 5B. The hallway suddenly felt colder.

Oscar shuddered.

"Maybe we could just go back?" Butterbean whispered. "We can leave the investigating to Mrs. Food."

"It's now or never, Bean," Walt said, trying to keep her voice level. The hair on the back of her neck was standing up. And she didn't even believe in ghosts.

Nobody moved. The freshly painted door looked much more ominous than it had earlier in the day.

Finally, Wallace cleared his throat. "I can't live in your aquarium forever," he said from his place on Butterbean's tummy.

Oscar sighed. "Wallace is right. If there's a ghost, we need to get rid of it," he said. "We can't do that if we don't go in."

"And there's a pretty good chance we won't die," Marco said, clutching Walt's hair so hard that his knuckles turned white. "Right?"

"Right," Polo said, swallowing hard.

"Unless we die of fright. Or it sucks the breath out of us," Marco went on. "Ghosts do that, right?"

"MARCO, sheesh!" Polo said, smacking him on the arm.

"I'm just saying!"

"Well, stop!" Polo glared at him and climbed up onto Walt's head, her jaw set. She held the key in the air. "We're going in."

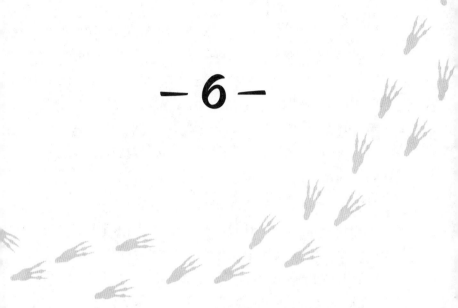

– 6 –

POLO TURNED THE KEY, THEN FROZE, LISTENING.

"Whew!" she said. "I was afraid something was going to—"

A thin wail filled the hallway.

Polo squeaked and pulled the key out of the keyhole, clutching it to her chest. "What is that?" she squealed.

The wail turned into a low, eerie moan. It echoed throughout the hallway and surrounded them. Butterbean felt the urge to howl along with it.

"GHOST!" Marco buried his face in Walt's fur.

"That's it! That's what I heard," Wallace shrieked, grabbing tightly to Butterbean's tummy hair. "It's the ghost!" He squeezed his eyes shut.

Walt stood wide-eyed, scanning the hallway. But no matter where she looked, she couldn't see anything suspicious. No ghostly apparition, no fog, no floating woman in a white nightgown, nothing. "Is it coming from inside the apartment?"

"It started when she turned the key," Marco sobbed. "It's the ghost."

"Bean? Anything?" Walt said quietly.

Butterbean sniffed the air, but it didn't help. She still hadn't figured out what a ghost was supposed to smell like. "I'm not sure."

Polo grabbed Walt's ears like they were game controllers and tried to turn her toward the elevator. "That's it. We're out of here. Wallace, you can live with us. Let's go." When the game controller move didn't work, she tried digging her heels into the sides

of Walt's head, like she was riding a horse. That didn't work either.

"Wait, what?" Marco said, peeking up through Walt's fur. "Wallace is living where?"

"Sorry, Marco, executive decision," Polo said. "We've got a roommate now."

"Polo. Stop." Walt tried not to cringe, but Polo had sharp little heels.

"Okay, sure," Wallace agreed. Anything was better than living in a haunted apartment or vent. "Let's get out of here." He let go of Butterbean's tummy and landed on the floor with a thump. Then he raced over to Walt, vaulting up onto her back in one jump.

Walt gritted her teeth. "Guys. Not a horse."

Oscar cocked his head. "Butterbean. Quick. Who lives on this floor?"

Butterbean looked around, her ears pressed back against her head. The wailing had turned into a shrieky cry that went straight through her skull and hurt her teeth. "Man Who Smells Like Onions, but he's gone. Next door is the Potpourri Couple, and the other two are Mechanic Guy and High Heel Woman."

Oscar frowned. None of them sounded likely to be making spooky ghost noises. "And do you smell anything helpful?"

Butterbean shook her head. She tried to block out

the sounds and focus on the smells. But it wasn't easy. "Nothing ghosty, I don't think." Butterbean leaned down and scanned the hallway. "Just hair spray smells from High Heel Woman. And potpourri, of course. And, wait—" Butterbean zigzagged across the hallway, muttering as she went. "Wait wait wait wait wait."

"WE CAN'T WAIT, BEAN! IT'S A GHOST!" Polo wailed.

"Okay, but I think . . ." Butterbean zigzagged over to the Potpourri Couple's apartment and sniffed a few times. "I think . . ." She glanced back over her shoulder at Oscar, took a deep breath, and knocked on the door.

The unearthly shrieks instantly stopped.

There was silence.

"Um. Yes?" A tiny voice came from inside the apartment.

"Ask if it's a ghost," Marco whispered, peeking through Walt's fur.

Butterbean took a deep breath. "Are you a ghost?"

"Who is this?" the voice asked. It didn't sound very ghostly. It didn't sound anything like Polo's impression from before.

"Butterbean," Butterbean answered.

There was no answer.

But then, just as Butterbean was giving up, the handle jiggled a few times, and the door swung open.

In the doorway stood a small white cat. "Can I help you?"

Butterbean shifted uncomfortably. "Are you a ghost?" She hadn't heard of ghosts answering doors, but she had to be sure.

"Do I look like a ghost?" The white cat looked irritated.

"Um . . ." Butterbean hesitated. The white cat sighed and then posed in a variety of prancey poses, like she was on a fashion runway.

Butterbean considered. "Kind of?"

"EXCUSE ME?" The white cat looked offended.

Walt narrowed her eyes and stalked forward.

"NOOOOO!" Marco, Polo, and Wallace shrieked

simultaneously, jumping off Walt's back and huddling around Oscar's feet.

Walt ignored them. She walked up to the white cat and poked it in the head with her paw.

"Ow!" The white cat reeled back a few steps.

"Solid," Walt said to Oscar. "Not a ghost." She turned back to the cat. "Okay, cat. What's with the noise?"

The little cat suddenly looked guilty. "Did my vocal exercises disturb you?"

"Vocal exercises?" Walt bristled. "VOCAL EXERCISES?"

The cat looked sulky. "Well, when my owners are away, I have to amuse myself, don't I?"

"But who are you?" Butterbean yelped. "The Potpourri Couple doesn't have a cat!"

The cat's fur puffed out a little. "They do now. I'M NEW. And you need to keep it down too. I could hear you talking all the way in my apartment." The cat turned, tail held high, and marched back inside, slamming the door with a kick of her foot.

"Well, there's your ghost, Wallace," Walt sniffed. "That explains the noises."

Wallace peeked out between Oscar's legs. "It doesn't explain the salt shaker."

Polo nodded. "Or the bathroom."

"Or the cupcakes," Marco added.

"THAT WAS ME, OKAY?" Wallace said. "I'M SORRY."

Walt frowned. "That's true. Maybe we should still check the place out?"

Oscar sighed. He could be in his cage right now, dreaming about the News. But the camera would be installed in the morning. "Yes. Our stakeout will continue."

"Sleepover," Polo said in a small voice.

"Stakeout, sleepover, whichever," Marco said, shooting a nervous look back at the cat's apartment. "Let's just get inside."

Butterbean stood up and pushed on the handle to Apartment 5B. The door swung open.

The animals peeked inside. Ominous shadows filled the room. "Or maybe we could just set up the sleeping bags in the hallway," Marco said, looking around anxiously.

The overstuffed floral furniture and knickknacks that had seemed homey during the day loomed menacingly in the moonlight, with dark shadows that didn't seem to be quite the right shapes, somehow.

Walt shuddered. Suddenly a sleepover seemed like the worst idea she'd ever had. And she'd had some bad ones.

Oscar clicked his beak. "Well, let's get this over with." He tried to get his bearings. He'd never loved flying at night, and that was even without ghosts to deal with. "I'll inspect the perimeter. Once we've established a secure zone, we can start the stakeout."

"Sleepover," Polo said in a tiny voice. "And about that. One quick question. Do sleepovers have lights?"

Oscar frowned. "I don't think so." He hadn't seen many sleepovers on the Television, so he wouldn't consider himself an expert. But since sleep was involved, it would stand to reason that the lights would be out.

"Okay," Polo said thoughtfully.

Silence descended on the room once again.

Polo cleared her throat hesitantly. "So another question. What about stakeouts? Do they have lights?"

Oscar fluffed his feathers. He'd definitely seen more stakeouts on the Television. He was back on secure ground. "I don't know if I'd say they have lights, per se—" Oscar started.

"Can we please turn on the lights?" Marco interrupted him. "This place is freaking me out!" He could swear that a shadow in the kitchen had just moved. And he didn't even want to know what that thing over by the sofa was.

"Yes, lights!" Polo squealed.

"Maybe lights will help us see the ghosts better,"

Butterbean added helpfully. If they were going to be taking sides, she was going to be on Team Lights. She hadn't wanted to say anything, but she'd spotted someone large and silent hovering just a few feet away. If she was right, this was going to be the shortest ghost hunt ever in the history of ghost hunts, because she'd totally found one.

Oscar sighed. "I don't think the ghost would mind lights, do you, Walt?"

Walt shook her head. "That should be fine." Walt tried to sound casual, but it wasn't easy. She was just glad the rats had been the ones to ask. The last thing she wanted to do was to play into the whole "scaredy-cat" stereotype.

Oscar flew over to the table by the door and switched on the light. It wasn't much, but it helped.

"Oh, ha-ha!" Butterbean barked in embarrassment, looking over at the looming figure nearby, which had turned out to be a not-a-ghost. "Nice coat rack. I knew it. Ha." She nudged Walt in the side. "See that? That's a coat rack."

Walt nodded. She'd seen coat racks before. She patted Butterbean on the back and turned toward the living room. Then she gasped.

There was a reason the shadows had seemed wrong. Nothing was the way they had left it.

The silver tray of fruit had been tossed on the floor.

One lemon had been partially eaten and then thrown so that it splatted against the wall.

And a trail of something red and sticky led from the kitchen to the living room, ending in a thick pool in the middle of the carpet.

Oscar flew to the edge of the coffee table and eyed it carefully, his heart racing. Ghost stories were supposed to be fun. They weren't supposed to involve dark red trails of . . .

"Is it?" Walt cleared her throat. "I mean, that liquid. Is that—"

Butterbean trotted over, sniffed it carefully, and then licked it.

"EEEEWWWWW!" the rats screamed.

"Cocktail sauce," Butterbean said, licking her lips. "It's cocktail sauce."

"What?" Walt followed the trail into the kitchen. The refrigerator door was gaping open, and there was a plastic tray on the floor.

"SHE LICKED IT WITH HER TONGUE!" Polo shrieked. Marco made gagging noises.

Oscar flew over and picked up a bit of plastic wrap with a label on it. "Shrimp cocktail with sauce. Tail on. Butterbean's right."

"Found one!" Butterbean said, nosing a shrimp tail

on the floor. The rest of the shrimp was nowhere to be seen. "Look, there are tails all over!"

"I don't think the cat did this, Oscar," Walt said. "She's not the ghost."

"Hmm. It doesn't look like it." Oscar cocked his head and listened. "But the question is: Is whatever did this still here?"

The animals froze, afraid to look into the shadows.

"Weren't you going to do a perimeter search?" Walt said, not meeting Oscar's eye. She didn't want to be the one to check out the other rooms, that was for sure.

"Yes." Oscar clicked his beak grimly. "I'll do the search. If it's safe, we should set up in the living room, I guess. If we're still doing the stakeout. Just keep away from the um . . ." He cringed, eyeing the red pool. "Stay on the couch."

Walt lashed her tail nervously. "Nobody touch anything," she said to the others. "We need to preserve the scene just as is for Mrs. Food."

"Urk, sorry," Butterbean said, spitting a half-chewed shrimp tail back out onto the floor.

"I'll do my sweep now," Oscar said, hopping from one foot to another. "I'm going. Sweep of the perimeter. Right now." He didn't move.

"Good plan," Walt said. Her whiskers hadn't stopped

trembling since they'd been inside. She hoped no one had noticed. "Oscar?"

Oscar sighed. "Going now." He took off and flew out of the kitchen.

Walt ducked her head down so the bag around her neck fell on the floor. "There you go," she said to Marco and Polo. "Sleeping bags. If you can sleep."

"Really?" Polo perked up. She scrambled over and grabbed the bag. "Marco, Wallace! Help me get this to the couch."

They dragged the bag to the edge of the couch, and then Polo opened it, sticking the top half of her body inside to rummage around. "OH, WALT!" she said in a muffled voice. "THESE ARE PERFECT!"

She emerged from the bag, tugging the edge of a sock.

Butterbean's nostrils quivered. "SOCKS?"

"Sleeping bags," Walt corrected, blocking Butterbean's path. Butterbean had a thing for socks. Walt didn't blame her. "Tonight they're rat sleeping bags."

"Are they your compression socks?" Butterbean whispered. Walt had stashed away a pair of Mrs. Food's compression socks a while ago. She was very attached to them.

Walt snorted. "Of course not. Those are too valuable. I got these out of the laundry."

"Nice!" Wallace held up a white sock with a

pom-pom on the end. "This one comes with a pillow!"

"These *are* perfect!" Marco said, climbing into his own pom-pom sock. "And we've got my snacks. This is going to be great sleepover." He caught sight of Oscar flying back into the room. "Er. Stakeout. As long as we don't get killed by the ghost," he added.

"Sheesh, Marco," Polo said, climbing into her sock. "We'll get that ghost first. Just you wait."

Oscar landed on the couch. "Everything looks secure. I saw no signs of paranormal activity. Also no intruders. But I have an idea. Wait here." He took off and flew in the direction of the kitchen. A few moments later he came back, his feet clutching various types of cutlery. "Just in case, we have weapons."

He landed on the couch with a thud. His wings felt weak with relief. He didn't know what he would've done if he had found an intruder. Or a ghost, for that matter. "Whatever it was, it's gone now. But if it comes back, we're prepared."

"Dibs on the spoon," Polo said, reaching out and grabbing a teaspoon. Once everyone had grabbed a utensil, they settled back to wait.

Walt curled up with her fork on one of the couch cushions. Butterbean set her butter knife down and started turning around in circles to make a nest. Then they all lay there in silence.

Well, almost.

"Sunflower seed, anyone?" Marco whispered. "I have extra."

No one wanted any sunflower seeds.

"Now that I've got my spoon," Polo finally said, the edge of the sock pulled up to her chin. "It doesn't feel as scary."

"I just wish we knew . . ." Walt trailed off, her ears pricking up. "SHHH." Her ears swiveled toward the sound. "Did you hear that?"

Six pairs of ears strained in the semidarkness. And then they heard it. It was an eerie dripping sound, so soft you almost couldn't hear it. It was followed by a low humming noise that started and stopped without warning.

"I thought you said it was all clear," Walt whispered.

Oscar's eyes were wide. "It was. I swear it was."

"The not-a-ghost cat next door?" asked Butterbean hopefully.

Walt shook her head. "I don't think so." She picked up her fork in her mouth. "Come on."

Slinking slowly, she tracked the noise into the heart of the apartment. The others followed as quietly as they could. (The rats had trouble controlling their utensils.)

When they got to the bathroom door, they stopped. "It's in there," Walt said. "The ghost."

Oscar braced himself. "Ghost hunters, this is what we came for. On the count of three, let's get him. One . . . two . . . THREE!"

Oscar threw the door open, and the animals rushed into the bathroom and skidded to a stop. Forks and spoons clattered to the floor.

Nothing could have prepared them for what they saw.

Oscar gasped and reeled back. "MR. WIGGLES!"

– 7 –

A STRANGE OCTOPUS WAS SITTING IN A TUB filled with bubbling water. Two of his tentacles were stretched along the back of the tub. He rolled his eyes.

"Oh, wonderful. FANS," he groaned, sloshing water out of the tub. He flicked water at Oscar. "Be a good little birdie and leave me alone, and maybe I'll have my assistant send you a photo."

"That's Mr. Wiggles," Oscar whispered. His eyes looked slightly glazed, and his beak was hanging open.

"How'd he get here?" Walt muttered.

"Who's his assistant?" Butterbean whispered.

"Who is HE?" Wallace asked.

Oscar collected himself and bowed slightly in

the direction of the tub. Then he turned to Wallace. "Wallace, this is Mr. Wiggles, the octopus currently missing from the City Zoo."

Mr. Wiggles was the star attraction at the City Zoo, or he had been until he disappeared. He was famous across the country for his crowd-pleasing antics—squirting water, doing clever tricks for visitors, performing daring escapes, that kind of thing. But he was most famous for his talent for picking winners in sporting events. He'd successfully predicted winners in the Super Bowl, World Cup, and Kentucky Derby for the last two years. He worked for herring snacks.

"CELEBRITY octopus," Mr. Wiggles corrected, stretching and flicking more water at Oscar.

"Celebrity octopus. Forgive me." Oscar didn't even seem to notice the droplets of water on his head. "World-renowned celebrity octopus." He bowed again. "Mr. Wiggles, it's an honor."

Mr. Wiggles shrugged all of his tentacles. "Of course. But if you're a true fan, then you know my name is actually Jerome. 'Mr. Wiggles' is a stage name," he said, making air quotes. "It's just a character I play."

Butterbean bit her lip so she wouldn't laugh. If Jerome was anything like Chad, he probably didn't have much of a sense of humor. She was totally going to try to get him to do more air quotes, though.

Oscar giggled. All of the other animals turned to look at him in shock. Oscar wasn't a giggler. "I can call you Jerome? Again, an honor."

Wallace sat down hard on the floor. "I'm very confused."

"Me too." Walt walked closer to the tub. "So, Jerome, what are you doing here?"

Jerome's eyes narrowed. "Who are you? I thought you were fans. Are you press?"

"We're not press," Walt said.

"I KNEW IT! What network are you with?" Jerome put a tentacle up in front of his face like he was blocking a camera. "Talk to my assistant. I'm not doing interviews."

"We're NOT PRESS," Walt said louder.

"We're residents," Butterbean said.

"And I'm a rat," Wallace said.

"Um, yes. That's all true. But it is a valid question," Oscar said apologetically, hopping up onto the toilet. "What brings you to 5B?" Oscar couldn't imagine how such a famous octopus could've ended up in the Strathmore Building. It just didn't make sense, logistically or otherwise. Things like that didn't happen.

Jerome shrugged and examined one of his tentacles. "You didn't happen to bring any shrimp with you, did you? Sardines? Herring snacks?"

"Um, no," Oscar said. "I apologize for the question, but have you been here long?"

"Weren't you scared to stay here?" Butterbean asked, peering into the tub. There were so many bubbles. "Were you afraid of the ghost?"

"Ghost?" Jerome gave a bubbly laugh.

"I think he *is* the ghost," Walt said in a low voice.

"HE'S A GHOST?" Butterbean yelped, scrambling back. "Are you the ghost?"

Oscar frowned. "Jerome is not a ghost. But did you cause the . . . untidiness in the apartment?" he asked. "We need to know."

"I helped myself to a few snacks, made myself at home. What's the harm?" Jerome said, waving a tentacle nonchalantly.

"What's the harm? You trashed the place!" Wallace was shaking. "WAS THAT YOU IN THE FISH TANK?"

"Delicious." Jerome made loud lip-smacky noises. Butterbean wasn't sure how he did it, since as far as she could tell, he didn't have lips. "When will that be restocked, do you think?"

Wallace clenched his fists. "You took my apartment!" Marco and Polo each put a hand on Wallace's shoulder, partly to comfort him and partly to hold him back in case he decided to charge.

"You freaked out Mrs. Third Floor!" Butterbean said.

"And you're kind of messing up our sleepover," Polo muttered under her breath. She didn't think this was how sleepovers usually went.

Jerome shrugged, making waves that threatened to overflow the tub. "I had to get away. Fans can be so demanding," he said, shooting a look at Oscar, who blushed.

"But how did you even get here?" Walt asked again.

Jerome leaned forward and looked at Walt carefully. "Are you sure you're not with the press?" He sighed. "My assistant helped with the accommodations. He can tell you— Oh, there he is!"

The animals turned to the door, but there was no one there.

"Ahem." A voice came from the sink. A voice they recognized. Chad.

"Chad's your assistant?" Butterbean yelped.

"I'm not your assistant. Stop saying that, Jerome." Chad looked a little stressed out. His tentacles were clenched, and he was turning darker and lighter randomly.

He chucked a package of shrimp over to Jerome. "I found some shrimp." He turned to Oscar. "Got it from some guy on three. Looks like he's planning a party."

"Man With Stinky Sweat Socks," Butterbean said knowingly.

"Wait, YOU KNEW?" Polo said, pointing at Chad. "WE SPECIFICALLY ASKED YOU!"

Chad rolled his eyes. "You asked about a ghost. You didn't ask if I knew about an octopus on the fifth floor."

Marco considered. "He's right, we didn't."

"Well, STILL," Polo huffed. "You should've said something."

"Sorry, rats," Chad said. He didn't sound that sorry, though. "Jerome is a buddy from back in my egg days. We keep in touch."

"Social media," Jerome said.

"He needed a place to stay, so I told him about this place." Chad shot a look at Jerome. "It's short-term."

"My stay is open-ended," Jerome said, shooting a look back at Chad.

"What was wrong with the zoo?" Oscar asked. "They love you there!"

"THAT'S what's wrong," Jerome said, absent-mindedly squeaking a rubber duckie. "I'm sick of all the paparazzi. All those people, gawking at me. I can't take it anymore." He opened the bag of shrimp and guzzled it in one gulp. "Do you know what they make me do? I have to pick football winners! And horse races! What, do they think I'm psychic?"

"Well, you do have an impressive streak going," Oscar said.

"Sure, but it's OBVIOUS who's going to win. Some of those horses have ridiculous names."

Butterbean frowned. She didn't see how that made it obvious.

"Yeah, not like 'Mr. Wiggles,'" Marco said, snickering.

Jerome shot him a frosty look.

"So you just what, took a cab? Came through the pipes?" Walt frowned. "Is this building connected to the zoo somehow?"

Jerome rolled his eyes. "Obviously not. I told you—I keep in touch with Chad on social media. I've seen the pictures of that human girl he rescued single-handedly a few months ago."

"I'm sorry, what?" That wasn't quite how Butterbean remembered it.

"So when I saw her next to my tank, I recognized her immediately and took my chance. I'm very good with faces." Jerome turned to Chad. "You should really remind her not to leave her water bottle unattended that way. It only took a second for me to slip inside."

"You stowed away in a WATER BOTTLE?" Polo gasped.

"How did you DO that?" Marco examined Jerome critically. He definitely looked bigger than a water bottle.

"Talent," Jerome said, and shrugged again (with less tentacle action this time). "Once I got into this building, it was only a matter of finding Chad."

"I told him this apartment was empty," Chad said. "My apartment was not an option."

Wallace looked around helplessly. "But . . . are you going to keep doing that stuff? Mrs. Third Floor is really upset. And I was living here," he said. "At least I was a tidy tenant."

"She'll deal with it," Jerome said dismissively. "Can you imagine how thrilled she'd be if she knew MR. WIGGLES was staying here? She's lucky to have me here. She could do worse. I'm obviously a step up from her last tenant."

"But . . ." Wallace frowned. "HEY!"

Jerome flicked water at Oscar again. Oscar flinched. "Now, you be a good little birdie and hand me that remote." He waved a tentacle in the direction of the sink. A remote control was lying on the countertop.

Oscar blinked in surprise, then hopped over to the remote and handed it to him. "Remote for wha—"

Jerome clicked the remote, and a television screen appeared in the bathroom mirror.

"THERE'S A TELEVISION IN THE MIRROR?" Marco gasped. "Wallace, you didn't say your apartment had a TV in a MIRROR."

Wallace looked dumbstruck. "I DIDN'T KNOW!" He scrambled up onto the counter and pressed his face to the mirror.

Butterbean stood up and peered into the tub. There were way more bubbles than there should've been. "Is this a Jacuzzi?"

"WHAT?" Wallace said, looking wildly between the mirror TV and the tub. And he thought he'd been living it up by watching movies on the couch.

"It's the News!" Oscar said, staring at the mirror in awe. "In the BATHROOM."

Jerome turned up the volume. ". . . no ransom

demands have been made. Zoo officials say that while it's true that Mr. Wiggles has escaped before, this time there have been no signs of him. And with the mayor's ceremony and Mr. Wiggles's next big prediction scheduled for just days from now, time is running out. I'm Cathleen Carlson, Channel Seven News."

Jerome clicked the remote off and tossed it into the sink with a clatter. "Let them worry."

"What's the mayor's ceremony?" Butterbean asked.

Jerome floated on his back. "Some stupid thing. I'm supposed to pick the winner of something or other. Who can remember? They can manage without me." He glared at them all. "Now if you don't mind, I'm trying to take a bath."

"Of course." Oscar bowed again at Jerome. Butterbean had never seen him bob up and down so much. "Forgive the intrusion."

Walt cleared her throat and shot Oscar a significant look. "Except . . ."

Oscar blushed and looked uncomfortable. "We'll see ourselves out."

"Oscar?" Walt lashed her tail. "Except . . ."

Oscar stared at the floor. "Except one tiny thing." He spoke slowly, like each word was painful to say. "We're really not set up for celebrity octopuses here.

This is Mrs. Third Floor's apartment. She's . . . well, she's a tad bit upset."

"She's FREAKING OUT," Wallace said.

"You need to leave," Walt said firmly.

Jerome rolled his eyes.

"Chad lives upstairs," Walt started. "Why don't you—"

"He can't stay with me," Chad said.

"Nope, no can do," Jerome said at almost the same time.

"You heard the News. They really miss you at the zoo. The whole city is worried sick," Oscar said. "It might be a good idea for you to go back." He couldn't believe he was saying this. The one time he'd met a real life celebrity and he was telling him to go away. "Something to consider."

Jerome shook his head. "Nope, sorry. I'm staying right here." He patted Oscar on the foot. "But look, since it's so important to you, I'll be good. No more messes, okay? I promise."

Oscar looked doubtful. "Really?"

"Sure," Jerome said. "Why not?"

Oscar shifted and looked to Walt, who shrugged. It's not like they could make him leave. "I'm sure it'll be fine," he said to Walt. "He promised."

Walt snorted.

"We should let him take his bath. Give him privacy," Oscar said. He didn't meet anyone's eyes as he turned and hopped out of the bathroom.

"I'll have my assistant get you a signed photo. Love you!" Jerome called as the others followed.

"STOP CALLING ME YOUR ASSISTANT." They could hear Chad's voice as they trudged off down the hallway.

"I think the sleepover is over," Walt said. "Any objections?"

No one objected.

Oscar nudged Walt. "You don't understand. That was MR. WIGGLES."

Walt bumped his side with her head (almost knocking him over in the process). "I get it. And it'll be fine. He'll probably keep a low profile from now on."

As they opened the door to head back to Mrs. Food's apartment, a burst of music blared from the direction of the bathroom.

"Low profile starting tomorrow," Walt corrected herself.

Oscar just hoped she was right. He didn't want to think of what would happen if she wasn't.

− 8 −

GETTING BACK TO MRS. FOOD'S APARTMENT
was a lot easier than they had expected. The hard part
was waking up the next morning. At least, Butterbean
thought it was morning.

"Come ON, Butterbean!" Madison whispered.
"Wake UP!"

Butterbean opened one eye. It was dark. She shut
it again. Definitely still time for sleep.

"Come on, dog! Don't you want to go ghost hunt-
ing?" Madison asked, shaking Butterbean again. "It's
a secret adventure!"

"WHAT?" Butterbean's eyes snapped open.

"WHAT?" Oscar fell off his perch. He'd had a

hard time getting to sleep after all the excitement and couldn't help but listen in.

It was definitely still nighttime, but Madison was dressed and moving around quietly in the dark. A secret ghost-hunting adventure could only mean one thing.

"Oh no!" Butterbean yelped, sitting bolt upright. "JEROME!"

"Good girl!" Madison said, patting Butterbean on the head. "We're going to check out that apartment for ourselves. Find out the truth!"

"OSCAR!" Butterbean yipped. She didn't know what to do. Madison wasn't supposed to be a ghost hunter too.

"Walt!" Oscar croaked, shakily climbing back up onto his perch. "Alert! Help!"

Madison felt around on Butterbean's collar to find the place to clip the leash. "You heard what they said. Animals are good protection against evil spirits. So you need to come too, just in case."

"WALT!" Oscar jumped onto the bars of his cage. "Butterbean needs backup!"

"SHH!" Madison hissed, freezing in place. She stared anxiously down the dark hallway toward Mrs. Food's bedroom door. "Quiet, Oscar!"

"Calm down, I'm on it," Walt grumbled from her

bed. She hadn't had a hard time getting to sleep. She stretched and shook her back leg. "Apartment key?"

"I put it back. Thank goodness I put it back!" Oscar felt a wave of relief wash over him. He couldn't believe how close he'd come to forgetting to put back the key.

Walt nodded and slunk over to Madison, rubbing significantly against her legs. "I'm coming too."

Madison looked down at her, frowning. "Not now, cat . . ."

"Protection!" Butterbean wuffled softly. Oscar was right. She definitely needed backup.

"Hmm. Okay," Madison said, scooping Walt up in her arms. "This is probably kind of silly, right? I mean, it's not like it's really a ghost, right?" She laughed a little too loudly. "Well, we'll prove it either way," Madison said before Butterbean could answer. She picked the key up off of the counter. "It's all up to us." Then she slipped silently into the hallway.

"This is going to be bad, Butterbean," Walt said, blinking in the bright lights on the elevator ride up. "When Madison sees that cocktail sauce, she is going to FREAK OUT."

Butterbean swallowed hard. Eating all of those

shrimp tails had been a bad idea. "Forget the cocktail sauce. When she sees JEROME, she's going to freak out."

Walt narrowed her eyes. "He said he'd hide."

"No, he said he'd be good." Butterbean looked up at her. "Do you think he will?"

Walt snorted. "Nope. No chance." She wished the rats had woken up. They could've tried to warn Jerome, at least. But it was too late now. Mr. Wiggles was on his own.

"Fifth floor," the elevator lady voice said.

The doors opened. Madison took a step out of the elevator and then hung back. "You don't think it's really a ghost, do you?" she asked in a low voice. She stared uneasily at the door to Apartment 5B.

"No. It's an octopus named Jerome. He's Mr. Wiggles," Butterbean said, wagging her tail in her most reassuring way.

Madison didn't pay any attention. Typical.

"I mean, there's got to be some explanation, right? Some non-ghostly explanation?" Madison said softly. She didn't sound convinced, though.

"It's an octopus. Mr. Wiggles," Butterbean said again. "You saw him at the zoo. You need to keep a closer watch on your water bottle, Madison."

Madison smiled weakly and patted Butterbean on

the head. "Don't be scared, Butterbean," she said. "I'm sure it's not a ghost. We're going to prove it. We'll go in, solve the mystery, and be heroes. Got it?"

"Okay," Butterbean said. This was going to be a disaster.

Madison put Walt down and marched over to the door, dragging Butterbean behind her.

"I can't look," Butterbean moaned as the door opened. She squeezed her eyes shut and waited for the screams.

There was silence. Then Walt cleared her throat. "Butterbean, open your eyes."

Butterbean opened her eyes. The apartment looked perfect. No cocktail sauce. No shrimp tails (although

Butterbean thought she deserved the credit for that). No sign of Jerome or Chad.

"What the heck?" Butterbean barked as she looked around. "Were we dreaming?"

"I know, right?" Madison clicked on a lamp. "It doesn't feel haunted to me. Not even a little." She put her hands on her hips and scanned the room. "Huh. You guys wait here." She walked down the hallway and disappeared into the bedroom.

"WHERE'S THE COCKTAIL SAUCE?" Butterbean said, her eyes huge.

Walt shook her head. "It was definitely here before. Maybe Jerome cleaned it up?"

"You mean maybe CHAD cleaned it up. CHAD. NOT JEROME." A grouchy voice came from the kitchen. Chad was sitting on the countertop angrily waggling his tentacles in the air. "CHAD must've worked his tentacles to the BONE!"

"Do tentacles have bones?" Butterbean whispered to Walt, cocking her head to the side.

"NOT THE POINT!" Chad said, waving his tentacles wildly. "Look at this. JUST LOOK. DISHPAN HANDS!"

"But he doesn't have hands," Butterbean whispered under her breath.

"AGAIN, NOT THE POINT!" Chad snapped.

He flung a soggy sponge at the wall, where it slid onto the countertop. "I am DONE. And now, if you'll excuse me, I'm going home to BED!"

Walt shot a look behind them. Madison came out of the bedroom for a second before disappearing into the office. "Thank you, Chad," Walt said softly. "We appreciate it, we really do. But where's . . ."

"Where's MR. WIGGLES? The CELEBRITY?" Chad folded his tentacles in front of him. They really did look a little red. "He's just where you'd expect him to be. NAPPING. In the TOILET." He snorted. "And don't worry. I put the lid down."

Chad gave one last huffy snort and slipped down into the sink without another word.

"I guess that's . . . good?" Butterbean said, standing up at the sink to see where Chad had gone.

"Maybe we really can trust Jerome," Walt said thoughtfully as Madison came back out into the living room.

Madison put her hands on her hips again and stared around with a puzzled expression. Then after a long moment, her face crumpled. "Well, guys, I guess this was a dumb idea?" She sighed and sat down on a footstool. "It doesn't feel haunted at all! I didn't see anything—no ghosts, nothing. And no intruder, either. And look!" She held her arm out for Butterbean to inspect. "Not even any goose bumps!" Butterbean looked. Madison was right. No goose bumps.

"So, I don't know," Madison said. "I guess we should just . . . leave?"

"Unless you want to look in the toilet," Butterbean said, wagging her tail sleepily. It had been a long night. "The toilet's a good bet."

Madison ignored her. She picked up Butterbean's leash and opened the front door.

"If there's a ghost, you'd think it would want to scare me, right?" Madison said as she locked the door and then pushed the elevator button. "I'm a prime target. So there must not be one. I just don't know how to prove it."

"You'll think of something," Walt said reassuringly. Madison ignored her, too.

The elevator dinged, and the doors opened.

It wasn't empty.

Butterbean wasn't sure who looked more surprised, Mrs. Power Walker or Madison.

"Oh, hello again! Can you believe I forgot these?" Mrs. Power Walker laughed and held up a box of dryer sheets. "I'd lose my head if it wasn't stapled on," she chuckled.

"Um. Right?" Madison got into the elevator, a confused look on her face.

Mrs. Power Walker gave Butterbean a sympathetic smile. "Long night?"

Butterbean sighed. "You have no idea."

Butterbean felt like she had just closed her eyes when it was time to get up the next morning. And staying awake was even harder—especially once Mrs. Third Floor showed up.

"And Bob came right over and installed the camera. I don't even have to be there—I can see everything just using my phone!" Mrs. Third Floor explained for the third time. She looked at her phone like it was the most amazing thing in the world. Then, with a loving pat, she put it back into her handbag.

"Madison? You okay?" Mrs. Food leaned over and shook Madison gently. Madison was swaying a little too far to one side, and there was a little bit of drool forming at the corner of her mouth.

Madison jerked awake. "I'm fine! Wow, that's crazy. A camera!" She blinked rapidly and forced a smile. It had been as hard for Madison to get up that morning as it had for Butterbean and Walt, but she hadn't had the luxury of falling asleep in her breakfast bowl like Butterbean did.

"If you're sure." Mrs. Food frowned.

"Yes, like I said, a camera! It uses an app. It sends me alerts and everything!" Mrs. Third Floor continued happily. It didn't look like she had any intention of going home. "I'm just feeling so much better today," she said, clutching Madison's arm as she talked to her. Apparently Madison wasn't going anywhere anytime soon either. "And yesterday, everything seemed so horrible. I was even thinking of calling those ghost men I've seen on the TV."

"Ghost men?" Madison said skeptically. She shot a side glance at Mrs. Food, who smiled blandly.

"Yes, the men on the TV who get rid of ghosts," Mrs. Third Floor explained. "I was this close to calling them." She lowered her voice. "But then, I worry about the publicity. Can you imagine if it got out? A haunted apartment would never rent!" She sat back and sipped her tea.

Madison took a cookie from the plate on the table, looking even more skeptical. "Are you talking about the movie *Ghostbusters?*" She looked from Mrs. Food to Mrs. Third Floor again. "I'm pretty sure that's not real."

Mrs. Third Floor laughed. "Not the Ghostbusters, silly. The Ghost-Finder Men. They investigate paranormal activity and measure it. They're scientists! They do research and expel ghosts!"

"The Ghostbusters," Madison said again. "From the movie. Who you gonna call?"

"No, these ghost men are on the TV. They communicate with spirits! They may even be psychic," she whispered, like it was a deep, dark secret.

"Oh, wait, are they on cable? They're plumbers or something? I know who you're talking about." Madison nodded.

Mrs. Third Floor frowned. "Nooo, that doesn't ring a bell."

Mrs. Food cleared her throat. "I think Mildred is talking about some men who have a reality television show investigating ghosts. They're local."

"Wait, THOSE GUYS?" Madison suppressed a snicker. "The ones who wave gadgets around and talk about spiritual vibrations or whatever? With the cheesy graphics? The public-access guys?"

"Yes! The ghost men!" Mrs. Third Floor said happily. "But I don't think I'll need them. I haven't had any problems today."

A muffled ding came from Mrs. Third Floor's large handbag.

"Oh, there, you see?" Mrs. Third Floor grabbed her handbag and started digging around inside, finally pulling out her cell phone. "That ding means that the camera recorded an interaction. It's motion activated."

She smiled conspiratorially at Madison and Mrs. Food. "I've already had alerts twice! The nice man in 5C went to work, and it recorded him waiting for the elevator. And then that woman in 5D took her trash to the chute." She giggled. "It's like I'm a spy!"

She peered down at her phone. "Now, let's see. . . ." She frowned. "That doesn't seem right. . . ." Then she let out a small shriek and flung her phone onto the floor.

"What? What happened?" Mrs. Food asked.

Madison bent down to pick up the phone. "What is it?"

"DON'T TOUCH IT!" Mrs. Third Floor screamed, and then pointed at the phone. "I can't— See for yourself!"

"Okay." Madison gave her a worried look. "But I have to touch it to do that." She picked up the phone gingerly, watching Mrs. Third Floor the whole time, like she was afraid she might explode. Then she stood up to examine the phone. "OOF! Cat!"

"Excuse me, kid," Walt said, jumping onto Madison's shoulder. "I need to see this."

"Narration, please," Oscar said.

Walt nodded and coiled around Madison's neck to get a better view.

"What is it, Madison?" Mrs. Food asked, getting up to watch the video.

Madison hit play. The camera was set up to show the doorway of Apartment 5B and the hallway just outside the door.

When the video started, the elevator doors were opening, and a pizza delivery guy got out of the elevator. He stood for a few minutes, looking around and checking a piece of paper in his hand.

"Pizza guy," Walt muttered.

"This early in the day?" Oscar looked puzzled.

"OOH, I want pizza!" Butterbean yelped.

"Shhh!" Walt hissed.

The pizza delivery guy in the video looked at the

door of 5B and, after consulting his paper one last time, knocked on the door. Then he put the pizza on the floor, turned, and got back into the elevator.

"Pizza's on the floor," Walt said softly. "Pizza guy's leaving."

"That's strange," Oscar said.

"Pizza on the FLOOR?" Butterbean said wistfully. "It's like a DREAM."

"So that's it?" Madison looked up at Mrs. Food. "The pizza guy?"

"No! Keep watching." Mrs. Third Floor's lip trembled.

Madison looked back down at the video and then gasped. She looked up at Mrs. Third Floor, her eyes wide. She started it again and handed the phone to Mrs. Food.

"Oh no," Walt said, looking closely. "Oh no no no."

The tiny phone video showed the elevator doors closing. And for a few seconds, nothing happened.

But as they watched, the door to Apartment 5B silently swung open. No one came into view. No one was there.

Then, so slowly you almost didn't notice it, the pizza box drifted into the apartment, as if it were floating a few inches off the ground. Once it was inside, the door shut.

No one ever appeared in the video.

It was like the door had opened and shut itself.

"Was that . . ." Madison swallowed. "Who opened the door?"

"It was the GHOST!" Mrs. Third Floor sobbed. "The ghost opened the door. It's still there!"

Oscar cocked his head and looked at Walt.

Walt narrowed her eyes. "MR. WIGGLES."

– 9 –

WHILE MRS. FOOD WAS ON HOLD WITH THE police, Madison attempted to console Mrs. Third Floor. (She was not successful.)

"It's not a ghost," Mrs. Food said, covering the phone with her hand. "I promise." Mrs. Third Floor didn't even look up. She just sobbed into Madison's shoulder.

Madison patted her tentatively on the back. "She's right. I don't know what it is, but it's not a ghost."

"Official Ghost Investigator meeting, now," Oscar said, jerking his head toward the rats' aquarium. Walt and Butterbean strolled casually over to the aquarium, trying not to look suspicious. Which was relatively easy, since no one was looking at them.

"We've got to warn Jerome," Oscar said once everyone had gathered. "This is a disaster. The police are coming! They'll arrest Jerome!"

Walt sniffed. "Jerome is on his own," she said, keeping one eye on the humans. "We warned him what would happen. ORDERING A PIZZA?" she huffed in disgust.

"Do you think there's any left?" Butterbean asked, trying to keep from drooling. Pizza was her weakness. "If there's pizza, I could go warn him. I don't mind."

Walt huffed again, louder this time. It almost sounded like a hairball. "None of us can go warn him, Bean!" she said. "Mrs. Food is RIGHT THERE. She'd see us if we tried to leave!"

Butterbean sighed. Walt had a point. It wasn't like she was the best at sneaking anyway.

Polo nudged Marco in the ribs. "We could go, maybe? We could use the vents, now that they're not haunted."

"It's my apartment," Wallace said. "I should protect it."

"Yeah," Marco said. "It's Wallace's apartment. He should go. We could just run up real quick."

"Plus pizza," Polo added. She didn't think she'd ever had pizza before, and she wasn't about to pass up the opportunity.

"Not our problem," Walt said, lashing her tail.

"But Walt, he's a CELEBRITY! If they catch him, he'll be in the paper for MONTHS." Oscar hopped from his perch to the side of the cage.

Walt glared at him. "Too bad! We already did our part!" She sat down, curling her tail around her feet. "We can't get involved. Look, once the police get there, they'll realize it's not a ghost and—URK!" Walt made a retching sound as she suddenly flew upward.

URK!

Mrs. Third Floor was standing over them, clutching Walt by the middle.

Butterbean reeled back a step in shock. She'd never imagined noises like that could come out of a mid-sized cat.

"I need this cat!" Mrs. Third Floor wailed, hugging a dangling Walt in her arms. "This cat will keep the spirits at bay. It's the only thing that can protect me!"

"You okay, Walt?" Marco whispered. Mrs. Third Floor had come out of nowhere.

"Blurg," Walt gurgled, struggling to get a foothold somewhere on Mrs. Third Floor's front. Eventually she gave up.

"Meeting adjourned," Oscar said, keeping an eye on Walt. He puffed out his feathers. If Mrs. Third Floor did anything to hurt her, Oscar was prepared to take a page from Walt's book and "go for the eyes," so to speak.

"So, should we go, then?" Polo whispered to Oscar. "Warn them?" It seemed like the perfect opportunity, since Walt was otherwise occupied.

"Hurry," Oscar said. He just hoped they were doing the right thing.

"The police?" Jerome scoffed when the rats gave him the news. He was sitting in the middle of the living room, eating pizza straight from the box. "OOOOOOH I'm SOO SCARED." He waggled his tentacles in the air when he said it. It was kind of rude.

"Well, you should be scared!" Wallace said, grumpily kicking a stray pizza crust out of his path. Celebrity or not, Jerome had made a real mess of the place. It didn't even feel like Wallace's apartment anymore.

"Look, we didn't have to warn you!" Polo squeaked angrily. "They know about the pizza, okay? They saw you! They'll be here any minute."

"Mrs. Third Floor is pretty upset," Wallace said seriously.

"What else is new?" Chad said, his mouth full of pizza. He was sitting in a sink full of water in the kitchen, glowering at them in between bites.

Jerome waved a tentacle airily. "There's nothing to worry about," he said. "I made sure I was camouflaged. There's no way they saw me."

"That's the problem!" Polo stomped her foot. "You looked like a ghost!"

"We saw it. It looked like the pizza floated into the apartment," Wallace said, surreptitiously licking a bit of cheese on the side of the box.

"They have a video," Marco said, gnawing on a piece of crust. He wasn't even trying to be subtle—he'd just torn the closest piece off. "It was pretty scary."

"Marco!" Polo said, pointing an accusing finger at Marco's piece of crust. "You too?" He froze mid-chew. "Give me that," she said, tugging at a piece of cheese and taking an angry bite. Then she turned back to the octopuses. "Now, move it, Wiggles!"

"Fine," Jerome said, stretching his tentacles out like he was just waking up. "I was full anyway." He started toward the kitchen, snapping his tentacle in Chad's direction. "Chad, take care of this mess. These rodents don't want us to have any fun at all."

Chad flung his pizza at Jerome, hitting him in the head. Jerome stopped short, folding his tentacles in front of him. "Really, Chad? Really? Throwing things? How mature."

Wallace looked from Chad to Jerome and then back again. "Did we come at a bad time?"

Jerome glared at Chad. "Fine, leave the box. I don't care. They know about the pizza anyway."

The elevator in the hallway dinged.

"Oh look, here comes the fuzz." He laughed. "As if they'd arrest someone of my standing. The papers would never let them live it down."

He moved across the floor, camouflaging himself as he went. He'd only gone a few feet before the rats couldn't even tell where he was.

"I'll never get over how creepy that is," Polo muttered as Jerome disappeared.

They heard voices in the hallway and a key being inserted into the lock.

Wallace grabbed one last piece of cheese and took off toward the couch.

"Polo, run!" Marco pushed Polo in the direction of the vent. "Chad, Jerome, hide!" He shot a look into the kitchen in time to see Chad sliding into a canister on the countertop.

The door to the apartment swung open as the rats made it to the vent behind the couch. They were safe. Marco just hoped Chad and Jerome would be too.

"Yep, that's pizza all right."

Officer Marlowe poked the box with her foot, like she expected it to get up and scurry away. It didn't.

Mrs. Third Floor and Mrs. Food stood a few feet away with Madison and Butterbean, watching carefully. They looked like they might make a break for the door at any moment.

Officer Travis glanced at the pizza in disgust. "And you say it just 'floated into the apartment,'" he said, waggling his fingers in a spooky way.

"You saw the video, Officer." Mrs. Third Floor's voice was frosty. "I didn't make it up." She hiked Walt up a little higher in her arms. Walt didn't even have the heart to meow about it.

"Of course not," Officer Travis smirked. He hooked his thumbs into his belt loops and looked around the apartment. "Floating pizza. There's a new one every day."

Mrs. Third Floor turned back to Officer Marlowe and then caught her breath.

"Is that . . . blood?" she asked tentatively, pointing a foot at a blob of red on the carpet.

Officer Marlowe squatted down and examined the blob. She touched it with one finger and then smelled it. "Pizza sauce, I think," she said, wiping her finger off. "Not blood."

"Boy, you think that's bad, you should've seen last night!" Butterbean said. That little blob was nothing compared to the cocktail sauce she'd investigated.

Officer Marlowe stood up. "Officer Travis will take the rest of your statement. I'll check the apartment for other signs of an intruder." She headed back toward the bedrooms.

"Blarg," Walt said, squirming uncomfortably. Mrs. Third Floor hadn't loosened her grip once since she'd first picked her up. And one thing was clear. Mrs. Third Floor didn't know the correct way to hold a cat.

"Do you need help, Walt?" Butterbean asked, straining to sniff at Mrs. Third Floor's legs. (Madison was keeping a pretty tight grip on the leash.) "Blarg twice if you need help. I could go for the eyes!" She'd never tried it before, but it sounded exciting.

Walt glared at her.

"Here, let me take the cat so you can show Officer Travis the video again," Mrs. Food said, reaching out as Walt meowed pitifully. Mrs. Third Floor frowned and clutched Walt closer.

"I've seen it already," Officer Travis said quickly.

Mrs. Food tugged lightly at Walt. "Mildred . . ."

Butterbean wuffled softly. She'd seen something like this before, only it had been at Thanksgiving, and with a wishbone, not a cat.

"Okay, that's . . . fine, I guess." Mrs. Third Floor reluctantly loosened her grip and handed Walt off to Mrs. Food, who gave a visible sigh of relief.

Walt curled into Mrs. Food's arms and quickly examined her midsection. She was surprised there wasn't a mark.

"Here, see?" Mrs. Third Floor opened her handbag and took out her phone, snapping her handbag shut again with a loud click. She held the phone up for Officer Travis. "Look at this video!"

Officer Travis didn't even look at it before pushing it away. "I've seen it. I know, unexplained pizza activity." He rolled his eyes. "It flew."

"Floated," Mrs. Food corrected.

"Whatever. I got it," Officer Travis said, examining his nails.

"But . . ." Mrs. Third Floor looked at her phone sadly. "There's video."

"Nothing suspicious in there," Officer Marlowe said as she came back into the room. "No sign of an intruder. I did wonder about the water pressure, though, so I checked it out. It's good."

"Well, that's something," Mrs. Third Floor said, turning back toward her handbag to put her phone away. Her handbag was standing open.

"Hmm." Mrs. Third Floor frowned and put her phone back inside. Then she snapped the handbag shut.

"Uh-oh," Butterbean said, eyeing the handbag. She had a bad feeling in the pit of her stomach, and there was no rat hanging there to blame it on.

"Unfortunately, there's not much we can do at the moment," Officer Marlowe said. "But if you'll initial right here, we'll file another report and let you know when we have any new information." Officer Marlowe handed her a pad of paper.

"Right," Officer Travis snorted.

"Yes, okay," Mrs. Third Floor said, shooting Officer Travis a look before taking the paper. "I just need a pen." She looked down at her handbag. It was open.

Mrs. Third Floor visibly jumped. She pointed at the handbag. "But I—I closed that!"

Officer Marlowe took a pen out of her pocket and held it out to Mrs. Third Floor. "What, the purse? Sometimes latches don't catch." She smiled. "Your initials?"

"Walt?" Butterbean said. Her bad feeling was getting worse.

"I know," Walt said. They both had their eyes on the handbag.

"Right, of course." Mrs. Third Floor closed her handbag again and took the pen.

"And I just initial . . ."

"Here." Officer Marlowe pointed at the paper.

"Of course." Mrs. Third Floor initialed the paper and then turned back to her handbag. It was standing wide open.

"AAIIIIEEEEE!" Mrs. Third Floor clutched at Officer Marlowe's arm.

A small snickering sound came from under the coffee table.

"JEROME!" Walt yowled, struggling to get away from Mrs. Food. "I KNOW THAT'S YOU."

"IT'S THE GHOST!" Mrs. Third Floor wailed. Officer Marlowe shot a look at Officer Travis. He was smirking.

A loud crash came from the kitchen.

Officer Travis was suddenly serious. He unhooked his flashlight and turned to Officer Marlowe. "I'll check that out. You take care of her."

Flashlight in hand, Officer Travis crept slowly and silently into the kitchen, followed by a slightly less silent Butterbean.

As he came through the door, he stopped short.

A small white figure hovered in the sink.

Officer Travis stood dead in his tracks and stared.

He didn't even seem to be breathing. All of the color drained from his face. Hand shaking, he pointed the flashlight beam at the sink.

The white figure raised what seemed to be a hundred arms and waggled them in the air before disappearing completely.

"URGH!" Officer Travis gurgled as he flung the flashlight at the sink, sending it clattering onto the counter. Then he raced over and looked inside. There was nothing there, just a fine powdery residue sprinkled on the countertop.

He quickly bent down, examining the cabinet under the sink.

Nothing.

"What was it?" Officer Marlowe called from the living room.

"Was it the ghost?" Mrs. Third Floor squeaked.

Officer Travis leaned against the sink for a long minute, then looked back into the living room, his eyes glazed. "Nothing. It was nothing." He picked up the flashlight and hooked it back onto his belt.

Officer Marlowe appeared in the doorway. "But what—"

"This is a waste of time," Officer Travis said abruptly, pushing past her into the living room. "We've got the report. I'm leaving. Waste of time." He lunged for the door and slammed it hard behind him.

Walt squirmed free of Mrs. Food's grip and streaked into the kitchen, where Butterbean was standing with her paws on the counter. Walt hopped up and examined the white powder as Officer Marlowe came in.

"I apologize for my partner. But please, ma'am, could you control your animals?" Officer Marlowe's voice was tight.

Mrs. Third Floor peered through the doorway. "What's that white stuff?" She gasped. "ECTO-PLASM?"

Walt sniffed it. "Flour."

"Was that Chad?" Butterbean asked softly as Madison hurried into the kitchen.

"Sorry about that." Chad's voice drifted up from the drain in the sink. "I picked a bad hiding place. It's all over me."

Madison picked the canister lid up off of the floor. "I think your flour canister exploded," she said, turning the lid over in her hands. Then she nudged Butterbean conspiratorially.

"Look, this is all super weird, right?" Madison whispered softly. "But I'm just not getting a ghosty feeling. Are you?" She looked at Butterbean with a serious expression.

Butterbean thumped her tail. It had worked last time, and she wasn't good at whispering.

Madison nodded. "Right." She took a deep breath and turned back to Mrs. Third Floor. "You know, that happens with flour A LOT, from what I hear." She shot Mrs. Food a significant look.

Mrs. Food looked puzzled for a second and then nodded like she was a bobblehead. "Oh yes, all the time," Mrs. Food agreed. "It's the . . . um . . . pressure. It just builds up. Right, Officer?"

Officer Marlowe sighed. "Sure. Tons of flour explosion reports. If I had a nickel," she said stiffly, patting Mrs. Third Floor on the back. "Nothing to worry about here." She held up the paper. "Thanks for the report. I'll be in touch."

Shooting a worried glance into the kitchen, she turned and hurried out of the apartment.

"It really was just a fluke," Mrs. Food said. "Bad batch of flour."

"Probably expired," Madison added.

Butterbean wagged her tail. Sounded plausible to her.

Mrs. Third Floor shook her head. "I don't care. I've had it. This is the last straw." She jutted her chin out at Madison. "I'M CALLING THE GHOST MEN."

– 10 –

MADISON COLLAPSED ONTO MRS. FOOD'S
couch. "She won't really do it, right? Call those TV
guys?"

"I don't know," Mrs. Food said, sinking down onto
the couch next to her. "Technically, it doesn't qualify
as a ghost sighting, so even if she did, I doubt they'd
be interested. But then, I thought the police would've
found the intruder by now, so . . ." She threw up her
hands.

They'd spent the last few hours helping Mrs. Third
Floor clean up after the police left, which meant they
cleaned while Mrs. Third Floor sniffled and hugged
Walt. It was a relief to be back home again.

"Sheesh," Madison said. She was too tired to move. She never would've expected ghosts to be so exhausting. She looked at the clock. "Oh shoot. Butterbean needs to go out." She didn't move.

"She can wait a little longer," Mrs. Food said, closing her eyes.

"It's okay, I used Walt's litter box," Butterbean said, trotting in from the kitchen.

"HEY!" Walt jumped onto the armchair, her fur bristling.

"Desperate times, Walt." Butterbean flopped onto the floor next to the rats' aquarium. "So what are we going to do? Are those ghost guys really going to investigate the apartment?"

Wallace poked his head out from underneath the cedar chips. "I don't want them there," Wallace said. "Don't I have any tenant's rights?"

Oscar gave him a sympathetic look. "Technically, I think you're a squatter," he said. "So no, not really."

"You should've signed a lease," Marco said, patting Wallace on what he thought was his shoulder. It was hard to tell with all the cedar chips in the way.

Madison cleared her throat. "So you think it's definitely an intruder?" she asked tentatively.

"Of course it's an intruder." Mrs. Food opened her eyes. "Nothing else makes sense. It's not a ghost, that's for sure. Why would a ghost order pizza?" She picked up the remote. "Let's see if we made the news. The publicity would just kill Mildred." She turned on the Television.

"OOOH! The News!" Oscar jumped up onto the bars of his cage to get a better view. He'd been feeling seriously News deprived. It had been almost a whole day. Anything could've happened.

"Look, it's Jerome!" Polo pointed at the screen.

There, on the screen, was a candid shot of Mr. Wiggles spitting water at a crowd of squealing zoo-goers. Then the image changed to a shot of a reporter in front of an empty tank, surrounded by sniffling and depressed-looking fans.

". . . and while the zoo has not found any signs of the missing octopus, officials say they have not given up the search. In addition, they are considering a wide range of options in the event that Mr. Wiggles is not found."

"What does that mean?" Polo asked. Marco shrugged.

"Wow, I can't believe he's still missing! Everything seemed normal there when I saw him," Madison said. "I wonder where he went?"

"He went with you!" Butterbean barked. "In your water bottle!"

"I've heard about octopuses escaping before," Mrs. Food said thoughtfully. "They'll probably find him hiding in another tank somewhere."

"Or upstairs! He's in Wallace's apartment!" Butterbean tried again. Mrs. Food turned up the sound.

". . . but without their star attraction, zoo attendance has reportedly dropped significantly. Back to you, Herb," the reporter on the screen finished.

"That's terrible. I hope they find him soon," Madison said.

"UPSTAIRS! He's in the apartment you JUST LEFT!" Butterbean made a face. She turned to Walt and shook her head. "I keep trying to tell her."

"I know," Walt said sympathetically.

"It's okay, Butterbean," Madison said, standing up. "You can stop barking now. I'll walk you."

"Madison, wait— look!" Mrs. Food turned up the volume on the TV. "It's them!"

A commercial featuring low spooky music had just started. Oscar peered closely at the Television. A slick-haired man and a bald man with a mustache stood in a room filled with lots of thick mist. It would've been spookier if the room hadn't looked like a condo in a sitcom. But then Oscar had discriminating tastes.

"And RIGHT HERE, in Agnes Nessman's OWN HOME, we were able to identify and communicate with three very agitated spirits." The two men waved their arms in ghostly ways while they talked. "And with our help, those uneasy souls have returned to their rightful place IN THE AFTERLIFE!" Thunder clapped onscreen.

Butterbean walked so close to the Television that her nose smudged the screen. The house where the ghost men were standing didn't look like it was haunted. And she didn't see any ghosts.

"Do the ghosts not show up for the commercials?" Butterbean asked after a second.

Oscar shrugged. "I wouldn't know," he said disdainfully. "This is not a show I watch."

"Tune in for a brand-new episode tonight on Channel Fifty-Seven. And don't forget," one of the men onscreen said. "There's no residence too big . . ."

"And no ghost too small," the other man continued.

"For the Ghost Eliminators!" they finished together.

The thunder clapped again. It didn't even sound like real thunder. (Butterbean would know. Real thunder scared the heck out of her.)

"That's them?" Madison took the remote from Mrs. Food and ran the commercial back. "They look like they work at a bank. And what are those graphics?"

Butterbean thought she must be talking about the squiggles of fake mist in the background. They were impressive, as far as squiggles went. But that wasn't saying much.

"Well, I don't know about that, but I can't imagine they'll be interested in Mildred's problem," Mrs. Food said, examining the frozen grin of one of the men onscreen.

"I hope not." Madison didn't like the looks of those guys. She didn't think they were serious scientists. "And you're sure it's not a fiction show?"

Mrs. Food turned the Television off. "Who knows? She'll never get hold of them anyway."

"Good. They creep me out," Madison said, going to get Butterbean's leash.

"I don't want those guys here," Butterbean said as Madison put on her shoes and jacket. "I don't like their squiggles."

Madison came over and clipped the leash to Butterbean's collar. "Come on, dog, let's get you outside before you make a mess." She shot a look at Mrs. Food and lowered her voice. "But first, we'll take a little side trip upstairs. We need to figure out this ghost stuff fast, before those creepy TV guys get involved."

Butterbean shot Oscar a panicked look. "Oscar?"

"Keep tabs on her, Bean," Oscar warned.

Butterbean nodded solemnly and trotted after Madison.

But as soon as Madison opened the front door, she took a startled step back. Because there, in the doorway, was Mrs. Third Floor. And she had a crazed grin on her face.

"Um, hi?" Madison stood for a second, unsure of what to do. Mrs. Third Floor didn't say anything. She just stood there grinning. Madison decided to try again. "Do you want to come in?"

"Good thing I used the box," Butterbean grumbled.

"What's going on, Mildred?" Mrs. Food stood up, smoothing her pants. "Have you heard from the police already?"

"Better!" Mrs. Third Floor burst out excitedly, waving a piece of paper in the air. It looked like it had been torn off of a yellow notepad. "I called the ghost men!"

"Already?" Madison yelped, shooting a look at Butterbean.

Mrs. Food's smile looked forced. "And?"

"And they'll do it!" Mrs. Third Floor did a little dance in the doorway.

"Oh crud," Oscar said, looking at Walt.

"Really?" Madison exchanged a worried glance with Mrs. Food. "For real?"

"For real!" Mrs. Third Floor cheered, happily clutching her paper. "I told them all about the apartment, and they were VERY interested. They're coming tomorrow!"

"Wow, tomorrow?" Mrs. Food looked stunned. "That fast?"

"That fast. They said time was of the essence with spirits." She looked at her watch. "Do you think there's time to go to the bank before it closes?"

Madison twisted the leash around her hand. "The bank? Why?"

"For their deposit, silly! But don't worry—they don't charge the full fee unless they find something." Mrs. Third Floor waved the paper again. "They'll even set up an installment plan for me!"

Mrs. Food frowned. She didn't like the sound of this. "How big a fee?"

"WHAT DIFFERENCE DOES IT MAKE? MY RENTAL IS HAUNTED!" Mrs. Third Floor screeched. Then she bent down and took some deep breaths. When she stood up again, the manic smile was back on her face.

"It's fine," Mrs. Third Floor laughed. "I'll just go in the morning."

Mrs. Food took a step forward. "Mildred. You're under a lot of stress—"

"Just have the animals ready. I want you all to come with me." Mrs. Third Floor squeezed Madison's arm. "Moral support. Okay?"

"Okay," Madison said uncertainly.

Mrs. Third Floor beamed at them and hurried out of the apartment.

"Um . . ." Madison looked at Mrs. Food, who marched into her office without another word. Madison looked down at Butterbean and unclipped her leash. "No point going now. We're too late," she said, shaking her head in disgust.

"Um. Walk?" Butterbean said as Madison disappeared down the hall. Butterbean looked up at Oscar. "Oscar? This is bad."

"I know," Oscar said, clicking his beak. "Walt? They're coming tomorrow."

Walt narrowed her eyes. "No ghost means no fee, right?" She stood up. "Then we just have to make sure they don't find anything." She turned to Butterbean. "Cover for me. I'm going to talk to Jerome."

– 11 –

WALT'S TALK WITH JEROME WAS NOT GOING WELL.

"But you can just stay with Chad! What's the big deal? It's for a couple of days, tops." Walt was so frustrated, she was spitting when she talked.

"Absolutely not," Chad said. "No."

Jerome snorted. "Like I'd stay someplace like THAT."

Chad glared at him.

"But don't you understand, there are going to be ELIMINATORS coming tomorrow." Walt tried to be calm. "They think you're a GHOST. They're going to charge money."

Jerome chuckled. "I think that's hilarious! Think

of all the fun I can have with them!" He wriggled his tentacles in anticipation.

"But money!" Wallace said softly. He'd insisted on coming along, since it was his apartment (and since he wouldn't be missed back at Mrs. Food's place). He didn't think Jerome was quite getting the problem.

Walt stared at Jerome for a long minute, considering. It was time for a new approach. "Think of all the terrible publicity when you get caught," Walt said finally. "So humiliating." She shook her head.

"You'd be in the tabloid papers," Wallace said, taking his cue from Walt. "But in a BAD way."

"Do you really want to get caught by those guys?" Walt added. "They're much lower level celebrities than you are."

Jerome drummed his tentacles on the countertop. "Hmm. True." Then he brightened. "But that's assuming I'll get caught, which I obviously won't. You saw how I handled the police!" He chuckled again. "Did you see how that one man ran away! And that woman screamed when I opened her purse!"

"That was Mrs. Third Floor!" Wallace squeaked. "Our LANDLADY."

Walt gritted her teeth. "Okay, that? That's exactly what you CAN'T do." She took a deep breath. "Look, stay here all you want, okay? I don't care what you do. But just take a break for a little while. Trust me."

Wallace opened his mouth to object, but Walt silenced him with a glance.

Walt got up and stalked over to Jerome. "When those ghost guys are here, you have to be quiet. Because don't you see? If you do ANYTHING to make them think there's a ghost here, they'll keep coming back. Again and again and again. You won't get a minute's peace. It'll be worse than the paparazzi."

Jerome shuddered. Chad rolled his eyes and examined a sardine tin on the counter near Jerome. It was empty.

"And don't forget the money!" Wallace piped up. "It sounds like they're going to charge Mrs. Third Floor a LOT." He felt like that was a really important part.

Jerome waved his tentacle dismissively. "I don't care about that," he said. "But I do want my peace and quiet. That's the whole point of being here!"

"Exactly!" Walt said. "So will you keep quiet? No tricks?"

"But that's so boring!" Jerome whined.

"Please?" Wallace said. "I'll even move out completely. The apartment will be all yours until she rents it out. Think of all the parties you and Chad can have!"

Chad snorted.

"Quiet parties," Walt added.

Jerome changed from dark to light a few times while he considered. Then he patted Walt on the head condescendingly. "Fine. No tricks."

"Promise?" Walt said skeptically. She didn't trust this octopus any farther than she could throw him (and that didn't seem like it would be far).

"Promise," Jerome said.

"And stop freaking Mrs. Third Floor out, too!" Wallace said. "She's been over A LOT. Think of Mrs. Food!"

Jerome made a face. "Look, I'll do what I can. But I can only be responsible for myself."

"What do you mean?" Walt narrowed her eyes.

"I mean this." Jerome reached out one tentacle and thumped on the wall. After a few seconds an unearthly wail drifted through the air.

"What the heck?" Wallace squeaked. "I thought there was no ghost!"

Walt groaned. "That's the prima donna next door, isn't it?"

Jerome nodded smugly. "So it's not just up to me, sweetie."

Walt lashed her tail in frustration. "Fine. If we can make her be quiet, you're in?"

Jerome smiled. "Of course." Then he snickered. "If you can work magic."

Walt stalked off without looking back. "Wallace? Time for stop number two."

"Have you seen the cat? She's not anywhere," Madison said, looking around the living room for Walt. She'd already been though the apartment twice, and it wasn't that big.

"Oh shoot. Oh shoot. Oh shoot," Butterbean muttered as she ran in circles in the living room. She did not have a plan to handle this. Walt had said to cover for her, and distraction was Butterbean's main covering technique. But for some reason racing around the living room was not working.

Mrs. Food waited for Butterbean to race by as she made her way to the kitchen. "Oh, you know cats. She'll show up when she's good and ready." She stepped over Butterbean as the dog rounded the turn.

"I guess. It's weird that I can't find her, though." Madison stood thoughtfully, stepping out of the way every time Butterbean made the circuit. "Maybe I'll look in the office again."

"Good plan," Mrs. Food said.

"Thank goodness," Butterbean said, collapsing on the floor as Madison left the room.

The rats burst out in a round of applause. "Way to go, Bean!" Polo cheered.

"Those circles were awesome!" Marco said. "I almost threw up!"

"Thanks," Butterbean said, blushing. Maybe she'd mix things up a little more next time. Figure eights would keep them on their toes.

Oscar eyed the vent nervously. He didn't think Madison was going to give up the search. He just hoped Walt would be back in time.

Stop number two was not going well.

"You do realize you're interrupting my valuable rehearsal time. And can I just add how rude it is to stick your head into someone's house uninvited?"

The white cat was sitting on a pink satin pillow in the middle of her apartment. Wallace and Walt had crept along the vents until they found the floor vent leading to her living room. And, to be fair, Wallace *had* stuck his head through the grate.

"Um, sorry about that," Wallace said, ducking his head back into the vent.

The white cat sighed. "No, it's FINE. You've destroyed my focus, so you might as well come in." She stalked over to the grate and swiped at it with her paw. The grate fell down onto the carpet with a thud. "I made a few renovations when I moved in."

Walt nodded approvingly. "I made the same reno-vation in our apartment."

Wallace wrung his hands nervously. Being in between two cats was pretty much his worst night-mare, and he just wanted it to be over. He didn't know why they were talking about decorating. He cleared his throat. "We came about your . . . um . . . singing."

"Yeah. Cut it out," Walt said, smiling a tight smile. "Please."

"Walt!" Wallace squealed. He'd been wrong about his worst nightmare. Being between two angry cats was much worse than being between just regular cats. He wished they'd go back to talking about the decorating stuff.

Walt sighed and then bowed her head a little. "Please," she said again. "At least for the next few days. We've got some visitors coming by next door tomorrow, and well, let's just say they won't appreciate your talents."

"They're not music lovers, I take it?" the white cat said.

"Those guys? Hardly," Walt smirked. "What do you think, Wallace? Are they music lovers?"

"N-no?" Wallace wished he could just go home. He didn't know why Walt was questioning him.

"No. They're eliminators," Walt said. "So if you could just—"

"If you don't mind," the white cat said, examining one paw. "I don't have time to listen to you talk about your social schedule. As it happens, I'm fully booked for tomorrow, so I wouldn't serenade your guests even if they begged me." She waved a paw at them. "You can go."

"Um, okay." Wallace turned abruptly and marched toward the vent. Walt put a paw on his tail and stopped him short. "Or not."

"Look, cat, this is serious. Do you promise?" Walt looked at the white cat through narrowed eyes. "No singing?"

"As if I would give a performance for free," the white cat scoffed. "Please leave me."

Walt started to go, but then hesitated. "That's a promise, right?"

The white cat looked at them for a long second. "You really don't recognize me?"

"Aw crud, another celebrity?" Wallace groaned.

The white cat laughed. "You're funny. Does this

ring a bell?" She stood up on her haunches and then waved both front paws in the air, meowing pitifully.

Walt and Wallace exchanged a confused glance. "Nooo?" Walt said slowly.

The white cat sighed. "Beautiful Buffet Cat Food?" She sighed again. "I've acted in almost all of their commercials. I'm retired now, though. You're one of the lucky few to see me perform off screen."

"Thanks?" Wallace said.

The white cat bowed her head at him slightly and then turned, tail high in the air. "Put the grate back on your way out," she called over her shoulder as she stalked out of the room.

Walt and Wallace looked at each other. "So I guess we're all set?" Wallace asked. "Since they promised?'

Walt had a bad feeling in the pit of her stomach. "I just hope you're right."

"And I had to run around the living room SEVEN THOUSAND TIMES!" Butterbean said when Walt and Wallace got back. "AT LEAST!"

"She was a great distraction!" Polo said as Wallace climbed back into the cage.

Marco nodded. "I couldn't watch anything else."

"You should've seen when she switched to figure

eights," Polo added. "She almost knocked Mrs. Food into the kitchen!"

Walt gave Butterbean a warning look. "Bean! You know she's fragile."

"I did NOT," Butterbean said, shooting an icy look at Polo. "I was very careful."

"Heads up, Walt," Oscar squawked, watching the hallway. "Madison's coming. She's been looking for you."

Walt nodded and hurried to her bed. She had just curled into a ball when Madison came back into the room.

"I still can't find her anywhe— There you are!" Madison said, walking over to Walt's bed. She stared at her for a moment with a puzzled expression on her face. "Have you been there the whole time?" She frowned. "I swear I looked there!"

Walt meowed at her sleepily.

"Weird." Madison patted Walt on the head and then stood up again. "Weird," she repeated. Then, shaking her head, she went into the kitchen.

"Is it all set?" Oscar asked quietly after Madison had gone.

"All set," Walt said. "When those ghost men get here, we'll be ready for them. Trust me, there will be no ghost."

She just hoped what she said was true.

– 12 –

BUTTERBEAN HAD A BAD FEELING ABOUT THE ghost men from the minute they set foot in the apartment, mostly because they almost stepped on her. And the worst part was, they didn't even really seem to notice.

"Watch the dog, please!" Mrs. Food said, scooping Butterbean up in her arms and examining her paw. Butterbean whimpered, mostly for effect. She was always up for a little sympathy.

"Oh yeah, oops. I was just overwhelmed by the spiritual presence in this apartment. I'm not surprised you've had trouble," the first ghost man said, brushing past her as he walked into the room. He had hair that was slicked back, and the smell tickled Butterbean's nose.

"Really," Mrs. Food said. Her voice was frosty.

"Yeah, it's super strong," the second man said in a bored voice, rubbing his bald head and then smoothing his mustache. He looked around the apartment like he was appraising the furniture. Polo considered hiding her button under a pile of cedar chips. She didn't trust these guys.

Oscar's eyes narrowed as he looked at the Bald Guy's head. "The common household appliance," he muttered under his breath. He would never forgive himself for missing that News segment.

"It must be quite a presence if you can feel it down here." Mrs. Food put Butterbean back down on the floor. "I'm Mrs. Fudeker. The apartment we told you about is upstairs. This is my apartment."

"Sure, I sensed that." Mr. Slick Hair nodded, shooting a look at the Bald Guy.

"No doubt," the Bald Guy said. "The whole building is probably a portal."

"That's exactly what I thought!" Mrs. Third Floor said. She held out her hand. "I'm Mrs.—"

"Mrs. Third Floor!" Butterbean barked helpfully. "Her name's Mrs. Third Floor!" Mr. Slick Hair shot her a nasty look.

"Oh, you don't need to introduce yourself to me," Mr. Slick Hair said, taking Mrs. Third Floor by the shoulders and gazing into her eyes. "The pain on your beautiful face tells me just who you are. It's your apartment that we're here to see."

"Oh brother," Madison said under her breath.

Mrs. Third Floor flushed and giggled. "Oh, well! Yes. It's my rental unit."

"Of course it is," the man said, patting her on the shoulder as he let her go. "Let me introduce myself. My name is—"

"You're Johnny Sims!" Mrs. Third Floor burbled. "I watch your show every week." She turned to the Bald Guy. "And you're—"

"Gordon Bailey. Right, now, let's get a move on. Wouldn't want anyone to get possessed, now would we?" He shot a nasty look at Walt, like Walt was plotting to possess somebody. Walt peeked back over her shoulder to check, but no, he was definitely looking at her. Her fur bristled.

Mrs. Third Floor's eyes widened. "Can that happen?"

The Bald Guy shrugged. "Happens all the time. We've seen it, what? Ten, twenty times?"

"At least. But we're here now. You have nothing to fear." Mr. Slick Hair smiled at Mrs. Third Floor.

"Good." Mrs. Third Floor leaned over and grabbed Walt around the middle. "I'm ready."

"URK!" Walt gagged as she was hauled up into Mrs. Third Floor's arms. She was never prepared for a scoop lift.

Mr. Slick Hair frowned. "You're bringing the cat?"

"Oh yes, she protects me. Madison, get Butterbean's leash. Let's go." Mrs. Third Floor looked like she was bracing for a fight.

The Bald Guy shook his head. "Whatever, lady. Let's get going."

"So you actually saw an apparition?" Mr. Slick Hair asked Mrs. Third Floor while they waited for the elevator.

"Yes, I did!" Mrs. Third Floor said, beaming up at him. Mrs. Food caught her eye and gave a slight shake of the head.

"Well, not exactly SAW," Mrs. Third Floor said slowly. "But there was the video—the pizza floated!"

"Yes, very intriguing," Mr. Slick Hair said. He patted his bag. "We brought some equipment to get some initial readings. That should tell us where we stand."

The elevator bell dinged, and the doors opened. It wasn't empty.

Mrs. Power Walker was standing in the elevator.

"Oh, hello there!" she said, looking down at Butterbean. "Brought more friends along this time, I see."

Butterbean wagged her tail in response.

Mrs. Third Floor looked confused. "Um, yes? There are a lot of us. Pardon me." There was a small stampede as everyone tried to squeeze into the elevator.

"Five?" Mrs. Power Walker's finger hovered over the button.

Butterbean and Walt exchanged a panicked glance. The last thing they needed was for Mrs. Power Walker to blow their cover. If she did, their days of exploring the apartment building were over.

"What? Yes, five. But how . . ." Mrs. Third Floor looked even more confused.

Mrs. Power Walker caught Butterbean's eye and shrugged as she pushed the button for the fifth floor. Butterbean lolled her tongue in response.

"Urk," Walt meowed pleadingly.

Mrs. Power Walker patted her on the head. "Nice kitty."

Then she winked.

"Oh yeah, the spiritual vibes are super strong here," Mr. Slick Hair said when they got off the elevator.

"They're just rolling off that apartment right . . . there?" He pointed at the white cat's apartment.

"There," Madison said, pointing at 5B. "It's that one. With the spooky ducky doormat."

Butterbean examined the doormat. She'd never considered the duck wearing a bonnet to be spooky before, but now that Madison mentioned it, there was something unnatural about it. As far as Butterbean knew, real ducks didn't wear bonnets.

"Of course," Mr. Slick Hair said, barely even looking at the duck. "I can sense a real presence here."

"Right," Mrs. Food said, unlocking the door. Then she stood back. "Voilà."

Mr. Slick Hair strolled inside, looking around thoughtfully. Butterbean peered in after him. It was quiet. If she didn't know better, she would never have guessed an octopus had been living there for the past few days.

"I'm feeling a really dangerous presence here," Mr. Slick Hair said, pressing his hand to his temple. "Super-strong vibes."

"You said that," Madison said, adjusting the leash in her hand. "Vibes of who? A ghost? Someone in particular?"

"I work best with silence, kid," Mr. Slick Hair said without looking at her. "Don't poison the atmosphere."

"Hush, Madison," Mrs. Food said softly. "Let them work."

Madison rolled her eyes.

The Bald Guy unzipped the equipment bag and took out a video camera and an elaborate-looking machine with lots of dials.

"So, do you need me to show you around? Or would that disturb the atmosphere?" Mrs. Third Floor hovered anxiously near Mr. Slick Hair.

He held out a hand at her. "Please. Let me take it all in."

"Um, I . . . okay." Mrs. Third Floor glanced nervously at Mrs. Food and pursed her mouth shut tightly, like she was afraid she'd keep talking otherwise.

"Walt!" Butterbean attempted to whisper (with limited success). "Do you see Jerome anywhere?"

"Blerg," Walt said as she dangled from Mrs. Third Floor's arms.

Butterbean took that for a no. Unless Walt could see something Butterbean couldn't, it seemed like Jerome was actually going to keep his word for once.

"Someone looking for me?" A voice drifted down from the light fixture overhead.

"Oh no." Butterbean was just in time to see a long tentacle drop down from the glass bowl covering the light. It dangled right over Mr. Slick Hair's head.

Walt made a sputtering sound. Butterbean held her breath, but luckily, no one seemed to notice the tentacle hanging from overhead. They were all focused on the Bald Guy setting up the equipment.

"JEROME! CUT IT OUT!" Walt hissed in a strangled voice. "NOT CUTE." Mrs. Third Floor

glanced down with a puzzled expression and loosened her grip a little.

"What's not cute? This?" Another tentacle dropped down on the side of Mr. Slick Hair's head and then moved around in the classic "I'm not touching you" style.

"HEY!" Butterbean barked. All of the humans turned to look at her. Mr. Slick Hair came within a whisker of touching the dangling tentacle but still didn't see it.

"JEROME!" Butterbean barked again so hard that her feet lifted off the floor. "You PROMISED!"

"You guys are no fun," Jerome sighed from overhead. "You're right. I promised. I'll be good." The tentacles shot back up into the light fixture.

Mr. Slick Hair shivered. "Did you guys feel that? It's like a spirit just went past. I could feel its essence next to my skin."

"YEARRRGHH," Walt growled, scowling fiercely at the light fixture.

"See? Even the animals sense it," Mr. Slick Hair said, glancing down at Walt. Walt hissed at him and then turned her bones to jelly and slithered onto the floor.

"No! Cat—" Mrs. Third Floor started, but it was too late. Walt had disappeared under the sofa.

"What kind of readings are you getting, Gord?" Mr. Slick Hair said. The Bald Guy fiddled with the machine and turned one of the dials. A sharp alarm sounded throughout the apartment.

"Sounds like we've got a ghost, Johnny," the Bald Guy said in a flat tone. Then he turned the dial back down. Butterbean sniffed his foot. (Just dirt.)

"Oh! That's a ghost alarm?" Mrs. Third Floor clutched her hands together.

"It sure is. You've got a very haunted apartment here. Verified ghost in here," Mr. Slick Hair said, patting the machine. "These machines never lie."

"Oh no!" Mrs. Third Floor clasped her hands so tightly that her knuckles turned white. "Can you get rid of it?"

Mr. Slick Hair nodded solemnly. "We can. But I'm afraid it won't be cheap, right, Gord?"

Gord shook his head and stuck his hands in his pockets. "These things never are, unfortunately."

"Wait, really?" Madison cocked her head. "I mean, really? A ghost alarm?"

Mr. Slick Hair turned and looked at her coolly. "So. You're a skeptic, is that it?"

"Don't believe in the other side?" The Bald Guy crossed his arms.

"It's not that. I mean—" Madison hesitated. Butterbean leaned hard against her leg and looked up at her with her best "something is up" face on. Madison frowned and then gave a slight nod.

"I mean, I guess I am skeptical?" Madison finally said. "It doesn't seem very haunted to me, that's all. And I don't see how that machine can tell if it is."

"That's it. Out." Mr. Slick Hair pointed at the door. "You're disrupting our readings."

"You mean the readings that just said there was a ghost?" Madison asked, her eyes narrowing. "So they're not accurate?"

"I can't work with her here. She needs to leave." Mr. Slick Hair turned to Mrs. Third Floor. "She needs to take that dog and go. They're disturbing the spirits."

"You should go, dear," Mrs. Third Floor said apologetically. "The spirits are getting disturbed."

"But . . ." Madison started, but Mrs. Third Floor was already pushing her toward the door.

"No arguments. We'll tell you what happens," Mrs. Third Floor said firmly.

Butterbean tried to dig her feet into the carpet, but

it didn't stop her from being dragged across the room. Not even when she flopped on her side and went limp. "NOOOOOOOOO!" Butterbean wailed as she and Madison were pushed out into the hallway. "It's up to you, Walt!" she cried as the door closed behind them.

Walt ducked down farther under the couch. The only thing visible was her eyes.

The Bald Guy cracked his knuckles. "Actually, the spirits don't like having this many people around," he said. "They should all go."

"Right." Mr. Slick Hair made a sad face at Mrs.

Third Floor. "I'm so sorry. You'll need to leave too. Both of you," he added, looking at Mrs. Food. "It's not me—it's the spirits. You understand."

"Mildred, I don't think . . ." Mrs. Food started to object, but it was no use.

Mr. Slick Hair put a hand on each of their shoulders and shepherded them toward the door, talking as he went. "We'll get better readings that way. And we don't want to anger the spirits. You just wait downstairs, and we'll let you know what we find out."

"Uh. Okay," Mrs. Third Floor said, bending down and looking under the furniture. "I don't know where that cat went."

"Forget the cat," Mr. Slick Hair said, gently pushing her out the door. "She'll be fine."

"If you say so. I'll just—"

Mr. Slick Hair shut the door in her face.

He waited, listening until he heard the elevator bell ding in the hallway.

Then he laughed.

"Think she's got anything good in the kitchen?" He sauntered into the kitchen, opening cabinets at random.

The Bald Guy snorted and flopped down onto the couch. "That type has everything. Take whatever you think the 'ghost' would want." He made air quotes.

Walt felt the hair stand up on the back of her neck.

This was really bad. Instinct was telling her to go for the eyes. She just wasn't sure which set of eyes to go for first.

"Are you going to go for the eyes?" The whisper came from behind her.

"AAAAAHH!" Walt jumped, slamming her head on the bottom of the couch. She whirled around. Wallace stood there with an apologetic grin on his face.

"Sorry about that. But I had to see what was happening! It's my apartment!" He inched closer to the edge of the couch to peek out into the room. The Bald Guy had taken out a pack of cigarettes and was tapping it against his hand.

"Oh no you don't, mister. Not in my apartment." Wallace clenched his fists. "You're going to stick it to those guys, right?"

Walt nodded. "I'm planning my attack."

"Well, don't take all day," a voice behind them said.

"AAAHHH!" Walt and Wallace both jumped this time (but Walt was the only one who hit her head. Wallace was too short).

Walt whirled around. It was the white cat from next door. "YOU!"

"What? Did you really think I'd miss the excitement? You never explained who your mystery guests were. Scam artists, am I right?"

"They're eliminators from Television," Walt said.

"OOOooo, do I know them?" The white cat peered out from under the couch. "Hmm. Not familiar. What program?"

"Ghost men," Wallace said.

"*Ghost Eliminators*," Walt corrected. "They hunt ghosts."

"Oh, LOCAL. Got it," the white cat scoffed. "I was in national ads. I don't know those guys." She licked a paw as she examined the Bald Guy's shoes. "Good quality, though," she purred. Then her eyes grew wide. "Now HIM I know! Is that Mr. WIGGLES?" Her voice went an octave higher.

Walt looked out into the room. Jerome had lowered himself down from the light fixture and was doing what looked like an interpretive dance in the middle of the floor. Neither of the men noticed.

"Jerome!" Wallace squeaked urgently. "NO!"

Jerome gave one last wiggle and then changed his color so he faded into the carpet.

"Is HE your special visitor? I didn't know you knew any celebrities!" the white cat said. "Besides me, of course."

"HE is not a visitor. HE is my roommate," Wallace said.

"SHH!" Walt hissed. "They're doing something."

She poked her head out from under the couch and swiveled around to get a better view.

Mr. Slick Hair had finished off Mrs. Third Floor's unlicked cupcakes and was brushing his hands off on his pants. Then he tossed the remote to the Bald Guy, who turned on the Television. He turned the volume down low, though, so you could hardly hear it.

"You got the camera ready?" Mr. Slick Hair said.

"All set." The Bald Guy turned the camera on. It was pointed at the corner of the room where the aquarium was set up.

"What are they filming?" the white cat asked. "If they need a model . . ."

"SHH!" Walt hissed. Mr. Slick Hair had moved into the shot.

"The spirits are gathering here, you can feel it," he said in a spooky voice. "Drawn for some inexplicable reason to this ordinary and shabby apartment."

"Oohh, she's not going to like that," Wallace whispered.

"If you listen, you can almost hear them calling. Their voices are coming from so far away, on the other side of the veil. Listen!" He tilted his head like he was listening. In the background, voices could be heard murmuring.

"That's the TV!" Wallace said, outraged. "Those voices are from the TV!"

Mr. Slick Hair shook his head. "The spirits are not strong enough to communicate with us yet. But their strength is growing." He jumped in surprise. "Look! In the corner! I can almost see an apparition starting to form." He pointed off toward the aquarium and then moved out of camera range.

"There's nothing there," Walt said slowly. "There aren't even any fish. What is he doing?"

"Thank goodness Jerome is playing nice," Wallace said. The last thing this show needed was a surprise appearance by Mr. Wiggles.

"They can't show a ghost if there's nothing there, right?" Wallace looked at the white cat, who shrugged.

"Beats me," the white cat said. "The sets I worked on were much more professional."

"HEY!" Wallace stood up indignantly. "Is he SMOKING?"

The Bald Guy had lit a cigarette, which he handed to Mr. Slick Hair.

"He's going to RUIN the upholstery. My couch will never be the same!" Wallace's whiskers were trembling. "MY APARTMENT ALWAYS SMELLS LEMONY FRESH!"

"Shh." Walt held out a paw to keep Wallace from rushing into the room.

Mr. Slick Hair took the cigarette and held it just

under the camera lens. Wisps of smoke drifted in front of it. "There, see? You can almost see the spirit attempting to materialize," Mr. Slick Hair said. "Those wisps of ectoplasm are signs that the spirit is present and wants to communicate."

"But . . ." Wallace frowned. "That's smoke."

"Trick photography," the white cat said. "Combined with those voices from the TV? It'll look great on film."

"Which they're going to show Mrs. Third Floor and Mrs. Food," Walt growled.

"That's IT!" Wallace punched his fist into his palm. "LET ME AT 'EM!" He raced out into the living room, heading straight for the Bald Guy. But halfway there, he seemed to reconsider. Instead he swerved around the Bald Guy's feet and jumped up onto the couch, hopping onto one of the remote buttons. The volume immediately shot up, so that the ghostly background voices were obviously from the TV. (It was a toilet paper commercial.)

"Walt!" Wallace screamed. He suddenly felt very exposed on the couch. "Distraction!"

"I'M GOING FOR THE EYES!" Walt launched herself out from under the couch and leaped up at Mr. Slick Hair's face.

But she wasn't fast enough. He saw her coming.

In one swift motion, he reached up and grabbed her by the scruff of the neck, so she dangled in midair.

"Get rid of that thing," the Bald Guy said. "That cat messed up the take. Now we've got to do it all over again."

"It's fine, we'll just double our fee." Mr. Slick Hair shook Walt. "How do you like that, cat? Double the fee sound fair to you?"

Walt tried not to react. She had to give Wallace time to hide. And if she twisted around just right, she thought she had a good shot of biting the man's hand off. (Or at least leaving a nasty mark.)

The man walked across the apartment, holding Walt out in front of him.

Wallace took cover under the couch.

"I'll go tell the others, Walt! It'll be okay, Walt!" Wallace's voice floated across the apartment.

Walt twisted in the air, slashing with her claws, but it was no use. She couldn't escape. She closed her eyes and tried to pretend she was a kitten again. It was so humiliating to be carried that way.

Mr. Slick Hair pushed open the bathroom door and, without a word, flung Walt inside. She spun around midair and landed on her feet as he slammed the door.

There was a round of applause from the sink. Two octopuses were sitting there watching her.

"She really stuck the landing, didn't she, Chad?" Jerome said, still clapping softly.

"Eight tentacles up," Chad said.

Walt shook herself off and glared at the door. "That man," she sputtered. "Those men—"

"Those men," Chad interrupted, "are even worse than you said."

"True. And I, for one, am offended by their stage-craft," Jerome said. "Well, you've convinced me. They've got to be stopped."

Walt slumped. She was locked in a bathroom, after all. "But what are we going to do?"

Jerome stretched his tentacles out in front of him and cracked them like he was cracking his knuckles. "What are we going to do? It's simple."

He looked at the door and smiled. "We're going to teach them a lesson."

— 13 —

"Do you think . . ." Mrs. Third Floor
hesitated. They'd been waiting for a long time, and
she'd started that sentence at least three times. "Do
you think . . . the ghost did something to them?" She
fiddled with the hem of her sweater. "Do you think it
could have . . . I don't know . . . eaten them?"

There was a silence. Madison bit her lip.

Mrs. Food cleared her throat. "I don't think that, no."

Mrs. Third Floor nodded and slumped in relief.

Butterbean sat bolt upright. She hadn't even considered that possibility. "OSCAR! Do you think
JEROME could've eaten them?"

Oscar picked through his food dish absentmindedly.

"Oh please. Do you really think Mr. Wiggles would do something like that?"

"Maybe not, but JEROME . . ."

"Jerome is still Mr. Wiggles deep down. He wouldn't eat them." He flicked a piece of browning fruit onto the bottom of his cage. "Besides, would you eat those guys?"

Butterbean shuddered at the thought of it, and she ate garbage. "Good point." She lay back down and put her head on her paws. "I'll be glad when Walt gets back."

"Me too." Oscar clicked his beak. He didn't want to say anything to Butterbean, but it made him nervous that Walt was still in the apartment. He just hoped she had something to report when she got back. And that it was soon.

"Why is it taking so long, then?" Mrs. Third Floor asked after a few minutes.

"They need to be thorough?" Mrs. Food said. "And maybe . . ." She patted Mrs. Third Floor on the hand. "They may be having a hard time finding a ghost."

"It probably really is an intruder," Madison said, scuffing the toe of her shoe on the carpet. "I mean, why would a ghost just show up now? It doesn't make sense."

"But the pizza . . ." Mrs. Third Floor started.

Mrs. Food held up her hand. "I know. But I still think there's some other explanation. We'll see what they say."

"Seriously, this is a condo building," Madison said. "Do you think a ghost would live in a condo? Like Bob would let that happen."

Bob was the maintenance man in the building, and he had some pretty strong ideas of how things should be run.

"I think Bob would take issue with a ghost living here," Mrs. Food said, smiling.

"You're right, he would," Mrs. Third Floor said, relaxing a little for the first time. "I'm probably being silly. Of course they're not going to find a ghost!"

"Of course not." Mrs. Food patted her on the arm again and got up to go to the kitchen.

Just as she did, the front door burst open, and the two ghost men rushed inside. (Without even knocking. Butterbean was shocked.)

"We got it!" Mr. Slick Hair patted his video camera. "Right here, we've got the evidence." He pointed at Mrs. Third Floor. "Take a look. You've got a ghost, lady!"

"Are you planning to stay in here all day, or do you want me to let you out?" The white cat pressed her face to the vent grate and peered down at Walt and the two octopuses. "Those two weirdos with the camera left ages ago."

Walt had been trying the door handle for half an

hour. It wasn't opening. All she'd managed to do was provide Chad and Jerome with free entertainment. They hadn't even offered to help. They'd been laughing nonstop.

"What do you think?" Walt hissed as she slid down the door for the fiftieth time. "LET ME OUT!" She was having a hard time controlling her temper.

"No, you can't go!" Jerome said, giggling hysterically. "You almost had it that time."

"Try that spin maneuver again," Chad said, struggling to keep a straight face.

"OUT!" Walt screeched at the white cat.

Jerome rolled his eyes. "Oh fine, you're no fun." He waved a tentacle at the white cat. "Let the grumpy cat out. It doesn't matter to me. Stop laughing, Chad."

Chad spit water at him.

Jerome turned on the faucet in the tub. "If those men are gone, I'm taking a bath."

Walt's eyes widened. "PLEASE, CAT! NOW!"

The white cat smirked down at her. "Just a sec." Her face disappeared from the grate.

Jerome tested the water with one tentacle and looked around. "I probably shouldn't use bubble bath, should I? Bad for my skin, I'd guess."

"Probably not?" Walt said. She couldn't imagine that bubble bath would be good for an octopus.

"Good thing the tub makes its own bubbles," Jerome said, turning on the Jacuzzi jets.

There was a thump on the other side of the door, and then it swung open.

"Oh thank goodness." Walt raced for the door. "Jerome, we'll have a discussion later. Make plans." She didn't want to stick around for a conversation. She just had to get out of there.

"Sure, sure . . ." Jerome said. Then he snapped his tentacles at Chad. "Chad! Get me some tub snacks, pronto."

Chad clenched his tentacles.

Walt didn't bother to see what happened next. She streaked past the white cat and into the vent behind the couch. She had to find out what was happening downstairs.

"See there? That's your ghost." Mr. Slick Hair pointed at the video on his tablet. "Right there."

"That's a ghost?" Mrs. Third Floor squinted at the screen. "It looks . . . well . . ."

"It looks like smoke. Is that smoke?" Madison asked, peering over her shoulder.

Butterbean stood up on the chair to get a better look. It wasn't easy to see, though. Mrs. Third Floor's head was in the way.

"It's a GHOST, kid. You've got a GHOST PROBLEM." Mr. Slick Hair leaned back and glared at her.

"It's always a shock the first time people see one, Johnny," the Bald Guy said, jiggling his foot as he sat at the table. He glanced at his watch like he had somewhere better to be.

"Right, of course." Mr. Slick Hair slicked his hair back and then wiped his hand on his pants. "Look, I don't want to be a jerk, but you don't have a lot of time to figure out what you want to do."

"What do you mean?" Mrs. Third Floor looked startled.

"We can get rid of the ghost, no problem. But we have to move fast," the Bald Guy said. "A nasty ghost like this, once it gets established?" He whistled. "You might never get rid of it. Didn't they have to demolish that one house, Johnny?"

Mr. Slick Hair nodded sadly. "Total loss. But unfortunately, the work we do? It's not cheap, especially with a rush job," Mr. Slick Hair said. "We'll give you a fair price, though. In exchange, we'll just need you to do some publicity for the show."

"PUBLICITY?" Mrs. Third Floor shot up like she'd been launched from a rocket. She scared Butterbean so much that Butterbean jumped back into Oscar's cage stand, almost knocking it over. "I don't want any publicity! I want this kept quiet!"

"It's not much, just a couple of interviews, a photo spread, maybe a commercial or two. Do you think that doorman out front will talk to us? Maybe some of the neighbors?"

Mrs. Third Floor grabbed the back of the chair. "No, absolutely not! Publicity would ruin me. Can't we do it a different way?"

Mr. Slick Hair shrugged. "I don't know. We do a TV show."

"We could make an exception, couldn't we, Johnny?" the Bald Guy said. "Since she's such a nice lady?"

"Oh yes, could you?" Mrs. Third Floor held her breath.

"Well . . . I guess so," Mr. Slick Hair said, after thinking about it. "Maybe we could blur out the identifying information?"

"We could . . ." the Bald Guy said slowly. "But you know the problem."

"That kind of technology costs a lot," Mr. Slick Hair said sadly. "And that's on top of our ghost elimination fee." He stood up. "I'm sorry. It's probably too much. We should just let you find someone else."

"NO!" Mrs. Third Floor grabbed his arm. "Please, I need you! It doesn't matter how much it costs—I can pay you. PLEASE!"

Mr. Slick Hair shot a look at the Bald Guy, who shrugged. Then he wrote something down on a notepad. "This is the lowest we can go with no publicity." He handed it to Mrs. Third Floor. She looked at it and swallowed hard.

"She looks like she's going to throw up," Butterbean said, watching Mrs. Third Floor carefully. She knew that look. "I hope she aims for the tile."

"If she does, she needs to clean it up," Polo said sternly. They'd had problems with barf on the floor in the past.

Mrs. Third Floor looked up at Mr. Slick Hair, her face grim. "I can pay this. How soon can you eliminate the ghost?"

Mr. Slick Hair shot a smug look at the Bald Guy, so quickly that Oscar almost missed it. But he didn't miss it. He frowned. He wished Walt was there to go for the eyes.

The Bald Guy stroked his mustache as he thought. "Like I said, you need to work fast with this kind of ghost, or it can be dangerous. We could do it maybe . . . tomorrow?"

"Oh yes, that's perfect!" Mrs. Third Floor clutched her hands together. "I'll be ready tomorrow!"

"But, Mildred," Mrs. Food said urgently.

Mrs. Third Floor waved her off. "No, Beulah, I have to do this. Tomorrow sounds fine."

"Great," Mr. Slick Hair said. "We'll take half up front, and half when the ghost is gone."

Mrs. Third Floor looked even greener than she had.

"She's definitely going to blow," Marco said, moving back behind the water bottle. It never hurt to be out of range.

"I—I don't have my checkbook with me at the moment," Mrs. Third Floor stammered.

"We might be able to make an exception this time," the Bald Guy said, heaving his bag over his shoulder. "You can pay us tomorrow. We trust you." He patted her on the arm as he headed for the door.

Mrs. Third Floor smiled stiffly as they left the apartment. Then she sank down onto the chair.

Mrs. Food locked the door and then turned, her face serious. "Mildred, I don't think . . ."

Mrs. Third Floor stared at the floor. "I don't have a choice." Her voice was flat. "No one will rent a haunted apartment, and I can't afford to have it empty. And if there's publicity? It'll be empty forever."

Mrs. Food took the notepad and looked at the number written there. Her eyes got wide. "But how can you afford that?"

"I can't!" Mrs. Third Floor's voice sounded strangled. "But I have to. I'll figure something out." She sat up and grabbed Mrs. Food's hand. "You'll support me, whatever I do, won't you? You don't think I'm being silly?"

"Of course I'll support you," Mrs. Food said. "You're my best friend."

"Thank you." Mrs. Third Floor slumped back in her chair.

Butterbean jostled Oscar's cage again. "Should we do something?" she asked in a low voice. "We can't let those guys do this, right? There's no ghost!"

Oscar peeked out through the bars. "I didn't think so. But did you see that video? That wasn't Jerome."

"No, it wasn't," Walt said, sticking her head out of the vent opening behind the couch. Her fur was matted and sticking out all the wrong ways. "It wasn't Jerome. But it wasn't a ghost." She crawled out into the room and shook off. "It was a fake. And we've got to stop them."

– 14 –

"WAIT, THEY PICKED YOU UP BY THE SCRUFF OF YOUR NECK?" Butterbean gasped. After Mrs. Third Floor had gone home, Mrs. Food had gone to her room with a headache, and Madison headed off to read in her room. It was nice not to have the humans underfoot for a change. Plus, it gave Walt a chance to fill them in on all the gory details.

"Like I was a kitten," Walt said, trying to keep her cool. She'd already told Butterbean the story four times, but for some reason, Butterbean kept coming back to that one detail.

"BUT THE SCRUFF?" Butterbean was shocked.

"That's so undignified," Oscar said, clicking his beak in disgust.

"Tell me about it," Walt said dryly.

"Wait, though." Butterbean was still trying to process everything. "You mean the SCRUFF OF YOUR—"

"YES, BEAN!" Walt snapped. It wasn't an experience she liked reliving over and over. She took a deep breath. "Look, it sounds worse than it was."

"Oh sure," a voice came from the vent. "Looked pretty bad to me. But what do I know? I'm just the one who rescued her." The white cat stepped out into the living room and looked around appraisingly. "So this is where you guys live, huh? More personal touches than the other place, I'll give you that. Kind of shabby chic. Emphasis on the shabby." She sniffed Mrs. Food's end table and curled her lip.

"Walt," Oscar whispered. "What's she doing here?"

Walt held up a paw at him. "Rescued is a pretty strong word, cat," Walt said, lashing her tail indignantly. "And didn't someone once say it was rude to stick your head inside someone's apartment uninvited?"

"Doesn't ring a bell," the white cat said. "Besides, what's the big deal? I don't see any humans around."

"That's not the point," Walt said, the fur on her neck bristling.

"I think what Walt's trying to say is WHY ARE YOU HERE?" Oscar said, hopping closer and eyeing the white cat carefully. "Surely we're not disturbing your vocal exercises all the way down here?"

"Pish," the white cat said, licking her paw.

"Oh no, did Jerome do something?" Polo asked from the safety of her cage. Not that she thought she was in danger, but there was a strange cat in the apartment. It didn't hurt to be careful.

"I bet he did. Is that it?" Marco made a fist and waved it menacingly. "I'll fix him!"

"Really." The white cat looked at them like they were hors d'oeuvres. "Well, since you asked, I came for the show!"

"What?" Walt said flatly. "What show?"

The white cat smirked. "I want to know the plan! Obviously, you're going to try to stop those men from scamming your human. And obviously, you're going to fail miserably. And I'm not going to miss a minute of it!" She settled down onto Walt's cushion.

Walt gritted her teeth.

The white cat stretched. "So tell me everything. What have you come up with? Some sort of physical attack?" She watched them expectantly.

"Don't be silly," Walt said, shifting uncomfortably. She decided not to say anything about going for the eyes.

"What, then? Trickery? Some sort of sabotage?"

Walt stared at her in cool silence. Butterbean did not.

"We haven't come up with ANYTHING yet," Butterbean said chattily. "We still need to come up with a plan. We've got NOTHING."

Walt shot Butterbean a dirty look. "Look, cat, what makes you think we'd—"

A squelching sound from the kitchen distracted them. It was a pretty repulsive sound, but one that Walt and the others had become all too familiar with.

"Who needs to be stopped? Jerome? Total agreement." Chad's voice came from the kitchen, his tentacles making a slippery sound as he slid down the counter. "He needs to go NOW."

"EXCUSE ME, but we're having a conversation here," the white cat sniffed. She turned to Oscar. "Mr. Wiggles needs to teach his help not to interrupt."

"HELP?" Chad's tentacles curled.

"But Jerome is your friend!" Polo said, climbing on top of the water bottle. "Isn't he? Don't you like hanging out?"

"FRIEND?" Chad scooted across the carpet toward them. "Do FRIENDS eat all of your sardines? Do FRIENDS snap their tentacles at you and make you adjust the thermostat ten times a day? DO THEY?"

"Um . . ." Polo squirmed nervously. She'd never seen Chad quite so worked up, and that was saying something. Chad was grumpy ninety percent of the time.

He wasn't finished, either. "Do FRIENDS demand that you spritz them with a mister when their tentacles start to feel crispy? Do FRIENDS erase your shows so they can tape MR. WIGGLES UPDATES? WOULD A FRIEND DO THAT?"

"Um, maybe?" Marco stammered. He shot a sideways look at Polo.

"HEY!" Polo squeaked. As if she would do any of those things.

"Maybe not that part about the shows, though," Marco added. "Or the . . . um . . . tentacles."

"I have TRIED to be a good host. I found him an apartment. I cleaned up his cocktail sauce. I ordered him a PIZZA! I AM NOT AN UNPAID ASSISTANT." Chad's tentacles were going wild.

"Wow, Chad. What are you going to do?" Butterbean sat down next to him, eyeing him carefully. He was changing colors so quickly it made her eyes feel funny.

Chad whirled around, almost smacking Butterbean with a flailing tentacle.

"What am I going to do? What are WE going to do?" Chad said. "YOU OWE ME." He pointed at Oscar with an accusatory tentacle.

Oscar ruffled his wings. "Er, I suppose . . ."

Walt shrugged. "He's right." There was no point in arguing.

Oscar nodded. "True. We owe you." Chad had helped them out more than a few times, and all he'd ever asked for was sardines. Well, sardines and unlimited access to Mrs. Food's kitchen.

"Okay, fine," Walt sighed. "We need two plans now. Plan Number One, get rid of the ghost men. Plan Number Two, get rid of Jerome. Anyone have any ideas?"

Oscar stared at the floor. Marco and Polo stared at the ceiling. Butterbean stared at her treat jar in the kitchen. No one met anyone else's eyes.

Walt sighed again. "Well, we have to move fast. We've got a deadline."

She looked at the white cat, who had folded her

paws and was watching them all with amusement. "Are you just here to gloat or are you planning to help?"

The white cat made a surprised face. "Oh, I can't imagine you need me. I'm sure you'll do very well on your own." She smiled smugly.

Walt clenched her teeth. "Fine. But you need to answer one question. Did you or Wallace see what the men did after I was . . . um . . ."

"Tossed in the bathroom like a rag doll?" the cat smirked. "I saw a little. But who's Wallace?"

Butterbean's eyes got wide. "Wait a minute. WHERE'S Wallace?" she asked, standing up and looking around like she might have accidentally squished him.

"He's not back?" Walt frowned. "I just assumed . . ."

She looked suspiciously at the rat-sized pile of cedar chips in the aquarium, which was apparently just a pile of cedar chips. "He said he was coming back here. He ran for the vent when I was . . . um . . ."

"Tossed in the bathroom. We know," Polo said helpfully. "Like a rag doll."

"He didn't come back here," Marco said. His eyes widened. "Do you think something happened to him?"

Oscar hopped up onto the bars of his cage. "Don't be silly. Wallace is fine. He must still be in the vents. He does live there, after all."

"No, he doesn't," Polo objected. "He lives in 5B now. He moved all his stuff."

Marco nodded. "I carried his collection of lost keys myself."

Walt felt cold in the pit of her stomach. "He said he was coming to tell you what happened. He was coming straight here."

"Well, he probably changed his mind," Oscar said. But as much as he hated to admit it, that didn't sound like Wallace. Wallace might be a wild rat, but he was practically a member of the family. Besides, he was part of their International Crime Syndicate. And as far as Oscar could tell from his Television programs, that meant they had an unshakable bond.

"That's it," Polo said, hauling herself out of the cage. "I'm going to find him." She hopped onto the floor.

"I'm coming too," Marco said, hopping down next to Polo. "He's sure to be somewhere."

"UNLESS JEROME ATE HIM!" Butterbean gasped.

"Jerome didn't eat anyone," Oscar said. He wished no one had ever mentioned that possibility.

"Oh, that's true," Chad said. "He wouldn't catch a rat himself. He'd expect ME to hand him one on a SILVER PLATTER." He folded his tentacles in disgust.

"Um. Sure," Oscar said. That wasn't what he'd meant

at all, but he didn't think this was a good time to contradict Chad. He'd seen those tentacles in action.

Polo marched toward the vent, making a wide circle around the white cat.

"I'm going to walk past you, visitor cat," she said. "So no funny business."

"Yeah, don't try anything," Marco said in his best tough-guy voice.

The white cat swished her tail as the rats scurried past. "As if I'd eat a RAT."

Polo made a strangled sound and started to turn back, but Marco grabbed her by the shoulders to keep her moving.

"Never mind her," he said quietly as they hurried into the vent. "I'm sure we taste terrific."

$$\twoheadleftarrow \twoheadleftarrow \twoheadleftarrow \twoheadleftarrow \twoheadleftarrow \twoheadleftarrow \twoheadleftarrow \twoheadleftarrow \twoheadleftarrow \twoheadleftarrow \twoheadleftarrow \twoheadleftarrow \twoheadleftarrow$$

Saying they'd find Wallace was one thing, but actually doing it was something else altogether. They had no idea where to look. And there were so many vents. They could be looking all night.

"Where do you want to start?" Marco asked, hurrying toward the nearest up vent. "Up? Or should we try down?"

"Up," Polo said. "He was coming from five. We'll retrace his steps." She tried not to think about the fact that Walt had already retraced them when she came home. It seemed like a bad sign.

"Good plan," Marco agreed, slicking back his fur.

They crawled up the vent and out onto the fifth floor, looking around carefully. The vents were silent and echoey, with the only noises drifting in from the various apartments. None of them sounded like Wallace sounds.

"Are the vents usually this creepy?" Marco said after a minute. He took a step closer to Polo. "I mean, they're always kind of creepy. But this seems extra creepy."

"They're just vents, Marco," Polo said, her whiskers trembling. The vents were definitely a thousand times creepier than they'd been before, but there was no way she'd admit it. "It's probably just because we've been talking about ghosts so much. That's all," she added.

Polo shivered. She wished she'd never mentioned ghosts. Because suddenly the idea that the vents could be haunted seemed like a very real possibility.

Marco nodded.

"Right," Polo said. "Let's get moving. He's sure to be in one of these."

"Sure," Marco said.

They didn't move.

"Okay, let's go," Polo said.

"Sure," Marco agreed.

They didn't move.

"OOOOOOOOOHHHHHHH." A voice floated through the vent.

"Was that you?" Polo squeaked. But she knew it wasn't. Marco's mouth hadn't moved. And besides, he was a lousy ventriloquist.

"It was probably just a—" Marco started.

"OOOOOOOOOHHHH," the voice said, louder now.

"A what?" Polo's voice was two octaves higher than usual.

"A—" Marco swallowed hard. "Just a—" He couldn't think of anything.

"OOOOOOOOHH WOW! OH MAN!" The voice was really loud now. And familiar.

Polo's whiskers stopped trembling. "Did it just say 'Oh man'?"

"It did," Marco said. "Also 'wow.'"

Polo put her hands on her hips. "That's no ghost. That's got to be—"

"WALLACE!" Marco yelled, running down the vent toward the sound, his feet completely unfrozen. "Is that you? What happened to you!"

Wallace rushed toward them, his eyes wide. He pointed back into the vent behind them. "Guys! Guys, you won't believe this. You've got to see. Check it out."

He dragged them down the vent to a nearby apartment grate. "LOOK!"

Marco and Polo peered inside. Then, after a few minutes, they turned to him, their mouths hanging open.

"No way," Marco said softly.

"Oh my gosh, Wallace!" Polo gasped. "Come on!"

Grabbing the other rats by the arms, she raced down the vent and dove into the down vent.

They had to tell Oscar.

And Chad.

− 15 −

THE THREE RATS RAN BACK TO THE APARTMENT as fast as they could. Polo even vaulted over the white cat in her rush to be the first to break the news. But by the time they got there, they were too out of breath to talk—they just collapsed in a heap in front of Oscar's cage. They'd spent the last five minutes doubled over, taking deep cleansing breaths.

"Issstteeeeeee," Polo wheezed.

Walt patted her on the back absentmindedly. "Any time."

"Take deep breaths, and try again," Oscar said patiently.

Polo nodded and did her best not to pass out.

Finally, the white cat stood up and stretched. "As fascinating as this is, I'll get the recap later. I have better things to do than watch a bunch of rodents breathe." She sniffed in the direction of the panting rats. "But believe me, rats, I will be back." She smirked at them and stalked off through the vent.

"Was that . . ." Marco huffed as he stood up. "Was that a threat?"

Walt rolled her eyes. "Of course not. You could take that cat down with one paw tied behind your back."

"Now, Wallace," Oscar said. "Why don't you start?"

"You should've gotten here way before I did," Walt said, her ears pricked forward anxiously.

"Because Walt was locked in the bathroom forever!" Butterbean said. "That fancy cat had to rescue her."

"What?" Wallace squeaked.

"That's not important," Walt said, shooting a look at Butterbean. "Just tell us what happened."

"Okay," Wallace said, puffing his breath out. He stood up straight and did a couple of stretches. Walt rolled her eyes. It was a little much, to be honest. He'd had plenty of time to catch his breath.

"When the ghost men went for Walt, I ran back to tell you all, right?" Wallace started. "But I wasn't looking where I was going, and I took a wrong turn somehow. I think I was panicking," he said sheepishly.

"We found him over by High Heel Woman's apartment," Polo said. "The one with the hair spray smells."

"And no sane rat would want to go THERE," Marco said solemnly.

"Because of the hair spray," Polo added.

Butterbean wrinkled her nose. She knew that hair spray.

Wallace nodded. "When I figured out where I was, I turned around to go back. But when I did, I heard them say his name. So I thought I needed to listen."

"Them who?" Butterbean had a lot of questions.

Oscar frowned. "Whose name?"

Butterbean nodded approvingly. That was one of them.

Wallace rolled his eyes, like it was totally obvious. "MR. WIGGLES."

Oscar cocked his head at Wallace. "Mr.—"

"It was on TV," Polo interrupted, bouncing up and clasping her hands. "They were talking about him on the TV."

"It was on the News," Marco added.

"Oh no, the News!" Oscar whipped his head around to look at the clock. "I missed it again!" He snapped his beak shut in irritation. This ghost situation had completely ruined his viewing schedule.

"What were they saying about Mr. Wiggles?" Walt asked. She didn't understand this obsession with the News. Oscar needed to find a new hobby.

"It was the man at the zoo," Wallace said. "He was saying . . . Well, it was crazy, so I didn't want to tell you all without being sure. So I decided to wait for the next broadcast. High Heel Woman always watches the News on both channels."

"THERE IS MORE THAN ONE NEWS BROADCAST?" Oscar reeled back in shock. Why had no one mentioned this before? How could he not have known? "Which channel?"

Walt shot him a look. "Just tell us, Wallace. What did they say?"

"The man at the zoo said they hadn't found Mr. Wiggles yet," Wallace said.

"Duh," Butterbean said under her breath.

"But he said if they don't find him in the next few days, it'll be okay, because . . ."

"THEY'RE REPLACING MR. WIGGLES!" Polo shrieked. Then she blushed. "Sorry. I just couldn't keep it in anymore."

"WHAT?" Oscar reeled back again. This was too much. He hoped his heart could take it. "How can they replace Mr. Wiggles? He's one of a kind."

"Well, not according to the zoo guy," Marco said.

"We watched the second News with Wallace, and the man said that—"

"YOU WATCHED THE SECOND NEWS WITH WALLACE?" Oscar's voice came out as a strangled squawk.

"Um, yeah?" Marco said. He hadn't thought that would be the part of the story that would get a big reaction.

"We found him right as the segment was starting," Polo explained.

"I needed witnesses!" Wallace said apologetically.

"Easy, buddy," Walt said, patting Oscar on the back. "Focus." She turned back to the rats. "He said that . . ."

Wallace nodded. "He said that they'd looked everywhere, and that it didn't look like they'd find Mr. Wiggles. So they talked to another zoo. One in Europe. And that zoo has an octopus they'll give them as a replacement. Monsieur Octavio. They call him the Annihilator."

"He's super famous in Europe," Polo said. "Everyone goes crazy for him there."

"He's like European royalty, according to the TV guy," Marco said.

Walt frowned. "So why are they willing to give him up, then?"

Polo shrugged. "They didn't say."

"Just being nice, I guess," Marco said.

A squelching, squeaking noise came from the couch. They all looked over just in time to see Chad erupt in laughter. "MONSIEUR OCTAVIO?" he sputtered. "THE ANNIHILATOR?"

Butterbean cocked her head. Bubbles were coming out of Chad as he laughed. She just wasn't sure what part of Chad they were coming from. "Is that his . . . nose?"

"I don't think octopuses have noses," Walt whispered, watching in horror. She took a few steps back. Chad was waving his tentacles in the air as he laughed. No one was safe.

"Chad is laughing!" Oscar said, nudging Walt in the side. "Have you ever seen Chad laugh before?"

Walt shot him a dirty look. She shuddered. "Yes. Yes I have." Although there weren't bubbles the last time.

"Monsieur Octavio," Chad sputtered. "As in LARRY? LOUSY LARRY? This is rich. Oh, Jerome is going to ink himself when he hears this." He sat straight upright and clasped his tentacles in front of him. "You have to let me tell him. Please let me tell him."

Oscar and Walt exchanged glances.

"Why?" Walt asked. "Is this going to make that big a difference to him?"

"He said he was happy in Mrs. Third Floor's apartment," Oscar added.

"He's sick of the limelight," Walt added. "Wouldn't leave if we begged him to."

"And we did," Butterbean added. "Lots of times."

"You want him to go?" Chad burbled. "You really want him to leave? Just tell him he's going to be REPLACED. BY LARRY." Then he laughed so hard he fell off the couch.

Oscar raised his eyebrows. "I think it's time we pay a call on Jerome."

When they snuck back to Mrs. Third Floor's apartment late that night, they found Jerome eating whipped cream straight from the can. Butterbean shook her head sadly. She could never get away with something like that. Foamy mouths weren't a good look for dogs.

"No, don't even try!" Jerome said, sending little flecks of whipped cream flying as he talked. "I'm not going anywhere. I've made up my mind. Ghost or no ghost, this is my apartment, and I'm staying put."

"My apartment," Wallace muttered, but nobody paid any attention.

"I'm gonna tell him," Chad said, a malicious grin

on his face. He rubbed two of his tentacles in front of him.

Jerome frowned and lowered the can. "Tell me what."

He didn't like the look in Chad's eyes.

Oscar shot Chad a nervous look. He didn't like it either. "There was a News report. The rats saw it."

"So?" Jerome looked uneasy.

"So they're going to REPLACE YOU!" Chad chortled. "WITH LARRY!"

The whipped cream can clattered to the floor. Jerome's voice was like ice. "What?"

"Well, it's not one hundred percent decided," Wallace said. "They're just talking about it."

"WHAT?" Jerome's voice was glacial.

"They don't think they're going to find you, see?" Polo said. "So they talked to a zoo in Europe, and they're going to get that octopus instead."

"Monsieur Octavio," Marco chimed in.

"The Annihilator," Polo added.

"LARRY?" Jerome roared. "LARRY THE ANNI-HILATOR?"

"Monsieur Octavio the Annihilator," Polo corrected.

"He's very famous," Marco said.

"That's right, LOUSY LARRY." Chad laughed uncontrollably. "FROM OUR EGG DAYS." He nudged Oscar, Walt, and Butterbean simultaneously. "Larry is the worst."

"So I gathered," Oscar said.

There was an uncomfortable pause.

Finally, Jerome slumped. "Oh," he said finally. "Larry."

"Um, yeah," Wallace said.

"So. What's Larry up to these days?" Jerome twiddled his tentacles anxiously.

"Just taking your JOB," Chad giggled.

"Keep in mind, it's not official yet," Oscar said, eyeing Jerome carefully. He didn't like the way Jerome was just sitting there, like he could snap at any minute. Oscar didn't want to be in range of those tentacles when he did. Standing next to Chad was bad enough.

"They're still looking for you," Walt said quietly. "They're still hoping they'll find you."

"They don't know you have your own apartment," Butterbean said.

"*My* apartment," Wallace said under his breath.

"Yes, well, they can keep looking." Jerome swept a tentacle to indicate the apartment. "THIS is what's important now. Not the fans, the adulation, the fame. None of that." His voice sounded flat. "Now it's just me in my apartment. Alone. With canned whipped cream." He gave a weird hiccuppy sound.

Butterbean didn't think that sounded all that bad, but then she wasn't famous. She nudged one of Jerome's tentacles with her nose. "You could go back if you want. We wouldn't be offended."

"Yeah!" Wallace squeaked. "And if you wanted to stay here sometimes, you could do that. We could share."

Jerome stared at Wallace for a minute, like he was sizing him up. Then he sighed. "No, that won't be possible."

"Why not?" Wallace thought he was being more than fair.

"Yes, why not?" Oscar clicked his beak. "JEROME! Be realistic! You can't live here—you know that."

Jerome waved a tentacle at them. "I see the problems, I really do. And I wish I could help."

Walt stood up. "The ghost men are coming tomorrow. We have to get rid of them, and trust me, we will. But the longer you stay here, the longer Mrs. Third Floor is going to think she has a ghost."

"Why can't you help?" Butterbean asked, tilting her head the other way. "It'll be fun! You can help us get rid of them and then go back to the zoo!"

"For that mayor thing," Polo said. "And the sports. They need you."

Jerome gave her a pitying look. "Yes, that all sounds nice, doesn't it? But it's just not possible."

"But WHY?" Wallace squeaked.

"Because," Jerome sighed. "I can't go back. I don't know the way. I'm stuck."

– 16 –

"So, we know what we need to do," Walt said while Mrs. Food and Madison were distracted by breakfast the next morning. "Plan Number One. Get rid of the ghost men. Plan Number Two, get Jerome back to the zoo," Walt said. "Any questions?"

Butterbean raised a paw. (It was a new thing she'd been learning with Madison. She was very good at it.) "I have a question about Plan Number One. What is it exactly?"

"I have that same question, except about Plan Number Two," Marco said.

Walt sagged a little. "I'm still working out the details."

Oscar sat on the bottom of his cage. It's what he did when he was feeling depressed. "We're doomed."

"We're not doomed," Walt said. "We'll think of something. We always do."

"Nice cheerleading, Walt, but it's too late. Look at the clock!" Oscar said, snapping his beak like the clock had personally offended him. "The ghost men will be here any minute. And what are we going to do? Even Mrs. Food can't talk Mrs. Third Floor out of hiring them."

Walt sagged even more. Oscar was right. "I'd just hate for those guys to win," Walt muttered.

"Me too," Oscar said softly.

Butterbean gave a mournful sniffle. "Mrs. Third Floor is going to lose her money, and Mrs. Food is going to be sad, and those guys are going to win."

"And Jerome is going to be in my apartment forever," Wallace added, sitting down next to her. He was going to miss having his own place.

"And Chad is going to totally lose it," Butterbean said. "I think he's got some issues with Jerome."

Oscar rolled his eyes. As if Chad's issues weren't totally obvious. "Yes, I think you're right."

The animals sank into a gloomy silence.

Madison took her plate into the kitchen and then tiptoed across the room to Butterbean.

"Bean. Psst," she whispered, shooting a look back into the kitchen to make sure Mrs. Food wasn't watching. Butterbean wagged her tail.

Madison squatted down and rubbed Butterbean's ears. "Look, here's the plan. When we go up to the apartment, I need you to keep your eyes open for anything weird. I have a theory." She shot another look into the kitchen. "I think this whole thing is a scam, and I think those TV guys are behind it."

"Well, close," Walt sniffed.

Butterbean leaned into Madison. "Don't worry. We've got our own plan. Plan Number One."

"Shhh, keep quiet, okay?" Madison said, eyes on the kitchen. "Just watch for anything sketchy. I don't know how they're doing it, but it's up to us to stop them. Okay?" She stared into Butterbean's face significantly.

Butterbean wagged her tail. "We're going to. I told you. It's Plan Number One. It will have details and everything." It was a secret, but Madison could probably be trusted. Especially since there wasn't anything specific to tell.

"Good," Madison said, giving Butterbean one last pat on the head. Then she hurried into the living room, doing her best to look casual. (She wasn't very convincing.)

"She's going to give the whole thing away," Walt

muttered, shaking her head as Madison clicked on the Television. It was the morning News.

"Hey, Oscar, check it out," Butterbean said. "News."

"Really?" Oscar peered through the bars of his cage. Then he stood up at attention. "Wait a minute!" He hopped up onto the perch to get a better look. "Wait a minute! Do you see that?"

An animated octopus was tap-dancing across the screen. It was wearing a beret. "Monsieur Octavio is known across the continent for his antics," the Television reporter's voice said. "And according to our sources, the two zoos are close to an agreement."

"Is that the replacement octopus?" Butterbean walked up to the Television and pressed her nose to the screen. "Wow, no wonder he's a celebrity!" She'd

never seen Jerome do anything like that. He didn't even wear hats.

"Butterbean, no!" Madison said, waving at her. "Back away from the TV. It's bad for your eyes!"

"Guys." Butterbean took a few steps back, just to appease Madison. (She wasn't worried about her eyes.) "Is that Larry?"

Walt hopped up onto the back of a chair and leaned forward, watching intently. The octopus on the screen whipped off his beret and replaced it with a top hat. Then, in a dizzying display, he started shuffling a deck of cards using at least six of his tentacles.

"WOW!" Butterbean said, inching closer. "Card tricks, you guys! Do you SEE that?" She looked back over her shoulder to make sure Oscar and the others were watching. "That guy is GREAT."

"That guy is trouble," Oscar muttered.

Walt frowned. "Butterbean, that guy is a cartoon."

"WHAT?" Butterbean whipped her head around so fast she almost fell over. "LARRY IS A CARTOON?"

Oscar closed his eyes. "No." Sometimes Butterbean was a bit much.

Walt sighed. "Larry's not a cartoon, Butterbean."

"But if that's Larry . . ." Butterbean said, frowning.

"That's just an animated version of Larry," Oscar said, not taking his eyes off the screen. "I'm sure the real Larry doesn't do tricks like that." At least Oscar hoped he didn't. If the real Larry was anything like the cartoon version, Mr. Wiggles had some serious competition.

He watched gloomily as the cartoon octopus balanced on one tentacle while holding sparklers that spelled out OCTAVIO. Then he gave an elaborate bow, and the picture cut back to the reporter.

"That was amazing!" the anchorman said, clapping. Oscar frowned. The anchorman seemed to have a lot in common with Butterbean.

"As you know, the zoo in Paris doesn't allow videotaping of their star attraction, so live footage of Monsieur Octavio is extremely hard to come by. But we were lucky enough to get a short video of the mysterious octopus. Here, for the first time ever, is our Channel Seven exclusive. Will this be the zoo's newest attraction?"

The video that started was grainy and dim, and looked like it might've been taken with an old cell phone. An octopus sat in the corner of a glass tank, curled up doing nothing. He looked more like a wad of used Silly Putty than the dancing cartoon octopus from before.

"Is he sick?" Butterbean inched closer. The octopus on screen didn't move.

An unsuspecting visitor strolled by the tank, leaned forward, and tapped loudly on the glass.

Without warning, the octopus erupted, launching himself toward the visitor in a violent display.

"WHOA!" Madison yelped, flopping back against the couch cushions.

"Holy cow!" Butterbean barked at the screen.

The visitor onscreen screamed and lurched back, stumbling and falling down out of sight. Larry curled back up into a ball.

"Wow. That sure was something," the anchorman said. Then he frowned. "Was he wearing the hat? I didn't see the hat."

"Good question, Herb," the reporter said. "And how is he at picking winning teams? We hope to have answers to those questions and more, coming up," she said as Madison started flipping channels randomly.

Butterbean turned around wide-eyed. "Boy, Jerome and Chad weren't kidding!" she said. "The real life Larry really IS a jerk!"

Walt nodded. She didn't like the looks of that octopus. She was no fan of Mr. Wiggles (and even less a fan of Jerome), but that octopus onscreen was bad news. She could feel it.

"No wonder they made that cartoon of him," Butterbean said, trotting back to Oscar's cage. "He was so boring before he freaked out. They have to make people think he's interesting so they'll come to see him."

"People believe what they want to believe," Oscar said sadly. He had a feeling Jerome was going to be living with them for a long time. It was hard to outdo a tap-dancing cartoon.

"He's got very good PR," the white cat said, sticking her head out from behind the couch. "He doesn't even HAVE to be interesting with publicity like that."

"Wha—" Oscar fell off his perch.

"SHEESH, CAT!" Marco squeaked, waving his arms in the direction of the couch. "Madison is RIGHT THERE!"

"SHE'LL SEE YOU!" Polo said, looking desperately between Madison and the white cat. Madison might not notice an extra rat, but an extra cat was hard to miss. Especially one draping itself dramatically against the side of the couch.

"It is customary to announce oneself," Oscar said, climbing back up onto his perch and smoothing his feathers. "To do otherwise is just rude."

"You can't just show up like that." Walt stalked over to the white cat. "You may not care if you get caught, but . . ." She trailed off and stared at the white cat thoughtfully. "If you get caught . . ."

"Go on?" the white cat looked at her with a bored expression. "Please enlighten me."

Walt turned around, a grin spreading slowly across her face.

Oscar stared at her, his feathers forgotten. "Walt?"

Walt lashed her tail. "We have a lot of work to do. Plan Number One is about to start."

Plan Number One was a lot easier to put into place once they actually knew what it was. They just had to move fast.

"So you know what you're supposed to do?" Oscar asked the white cat, who was not following instructions and moving fast. (She was doing some casual smoothing of her whiskers instead.)

"Sure, sure. I'm a pro, remember?" She gave her whiskers one final pat. "But just so you know, you're going to owe me. Big time." She stood up and turned with a dramatic flourish.

"Yes, I know," Oscar said, his heart sinking as she stalked into the vent opening behind the couch. He had a feeling she wasn't going to be satisfied with a few cans of sardines.

Walt jumped down from the arm of the couch and landed right in front of him. Oscar gave an undignified squawk. He couldn't take any more surprises. He puffed his feathers in irritation. "So? Did you do it?"

Walt smiled smugly. "I handled it."

"You made the phone call? It's all set?" Oscar just wanted to be sure. They couldn't afford any slip ups.

Walt shot him an icy look. "I made the call. It's done. We're all set." Oscar had to admit, Walt was very good on the phone. She had a computer program that she could use to simulate a human voice. Oscar could speak Human too, but in sticky situations, the computer voice was more effective. (It was good enough to fool Butterbean.)

"I just hope this all works," Oscar said, smoothing his feathers back down. They'd hardly had a chance

to think through all the details of the plot, much less troubleshoot them.

"It will," Walt said. She patted him carefully on the back.

"How do you know?" Oscar asked.

"Because it has to."

Oscar nodded. That made a certain kind of sense. He turned back to the vent just in time to see Wallace come streaking out.

"I did it!" Wallace shouted as he ran up.

"Mission complete?" he asked.

"Yes, complete!" Wallace squeaked, leaning on the side of Oscar's cage to catch his breath. "I mean, not complete YET, since we haven't done it. But I told him. I mean, them. I mean, I told Jerome and Chad what they need to do."

Oscar nodded. "And they agreed?"

"Oh yeah," Wallace said. "Especially once I told Jerome about that cartoon octopus on the News. Boy, was he mad."

"Good," Oscar said thoughtfully. A mad Jerome would be a motivated Jerome. And that's what they needed right now.

The doorbell rang. Oscar felt a rush of adrenaline. This was it.

"Okay, everybody. Places!" he said, hopping up into his cage and holding the door closed with his foot. Mrs. Food didn't need to know he could come and go as he pleased.

Mrs. Food hurried into the living room and opened the door. But it wasn't the ghost men. It was Mrs. Third Floor.

"False alarm," Oscar said, letting his door swing open a little.

"Shoot!" Butterbean barked. "Let's get this show on the road!" Butterbean's role in the plan was "stare at a fixed point in space and whine" and "backup as needed" and she was ready to get started. She was great at backing up.

Mrs. Third Floor's eyes were red, and her face was blotchy. "Well, let's get this show on the road," she said weakly.

Butterbean's eyes widened. "That's what I said!"

"Come inside, Mildred. I'm sure they'll be here soon," Mrs. Food said. "But are you sure you want to go through with this? You can still call it off, and honestly, I think you should."

Mrs. Third Floor didn't say anything. She just shook her head.

Mrs. Food patted her tentatively on the shoulder. "If you're still convinced it's a ghost, we can get some of that stuff that you burn. What is that stuff . . ."

"Sage," Madison said, coming into the living room. "It's sage that you burn. I saw it on TV."

"Madison!" Mrs. Third Floor smiled weakly in surprise. "You're skipping school for me? What a thoughtful gesture."

"Um." Madison shot a look at Mrs. Food. "Teacher workday, actually. But I totally would've skipped."

Mrs. Third Floor nodded distractedly and patted Madison on the arm. "That's nice."

"We can get that sage stuff to purify the apartment," Madison went on. "And we can call a priest if you want. We don't need those guys to get rid of a ghost."

"That's a wonderful idea!" Mrs. Food nodded encouragingly. "A priest! Doesn't that sound good?"

"I could go for sage," Wallace said thoughtfully. "It can't smell that terrible, right?"

Butterbean shrugged. She didn't know which smell was sage.

"And it'll be cheaper," Madison said.

Mrs. Third Floor shook her head again. "You know that won't work." Her voice was flat. "You heard the ghost men. They're the only ones who can get rid of the ghost. I don't have a choice."

"But, Mildred, how are you going to pay for this?" Mrs. Food said gently. "It's too expensive."

"I thought about that. I'm going to . . ." Mrs. Third Floor swallowed hard. "I'm going to have to put my apartment on the market. I'll have to sell. It's the only way."

"But you said no one will buy a haunted apartment," Madison said.

Mrs. Third Floor shot her a tight smile. "I know

that. They won't. That's why I'm going to sell my apartment on three."

Mrs. Food gasped. "But that's where you live!"

"I talked to my sister in St. Louis, and I can move in with her." Mrs. Third Floor gave a chokey sob. "I'll miss you both. But I don't have a choice. I'll use the money from my apartment on three to pay the ghost men, and once the ghost is gone, I'll sell the haunted one too."

"But, Mildred!" Mrs. Food looked shocked.

"But then she won't be Mrs. Third Floor!" Butterbean yelped.

"Mrs. St. Louis doesn't sound right at all!" Polo said from under a pile of cedar chips.

Marco poked his nose out too. "Mrs. St. Louis sounds bad," he agreed. "She can't move out!"

"Maybe you could just move to five? To the haunted rental?" Madison said, looking between Mrs. Third Floor and Mrs. Food and then back again. Mrs. Food had gone very pale. "Since it won't be haunted then, right?"

"I'm okay with that," Wallace said sadly. He hated to lose his apartment, but it would be even worse for Mrs. Food to lose her friend. He could probably find a different apartment. Plus, it hadn't been the same since Jerome moved in.

"Mrs. Fifth Floor doesn't sound nearly as bad as Mrs. St. Louis," Butterbean said thoughtfully. "It could work."

"Oh no, that won't work," Mrs. Third Floor said, her voice cracking. "I couldn't stand to see someone else living in my beautiful third-floor apartment!"

Mrs. Food pressed her mouth into a thin line. "That's it. No," she said grimly. "I can't let you throw your money away like this. It's not right."

Mrs. Third Floor glared at her. "It's not your choice, Beulah."

There was a knock at the door. "Anyway, it's too late. Here they are," Mrs. Third Floor sniffed, turning her back on Mrs. Food.

She threw the door open in one swift motion and then jerked back in surprise. It wasn't the ghost men. It was Officer Marlowe.

"Nice work, Walt," Oscar said under his breath.

Plan Number One had started.

— 17 —

"AM I TOO LATE?" OFFICER MARLOWE SAID, peering around Mrs. Third Floor into the apartment. She was wearing a faded madras shirt and jeans instead of her uniform, and it took Mrs. Third Floor a second to recognize her.

"L-late?" Mrs. Third Floor stammered. "Late for what?"

"For the exorcism, or whatever. Did I miss it?" She stepped into the apartment, edging past Mrs. Third Floor, who seemed rooted to the spot. "I'd hate to miss a chance to see the Ghost Eliminators."

"Oh, of course!" Mrs. Third Floor looked at Mrs. Food with a panicked expression. "I didn't realize you were coming."

Mrs. Food looked at Madison with a raised eyebrow. "Madison?"

"What? I didn't . . ." Madison turned bright red.

"Let's just say a little birdie told me," Officer Marlowe said, winking.

All of the animals turned to look at Oscar.

"Well, that's not true," Oscar said, shifting uncomfortably under the attention. "We all know it was Walt."

Walt shrugged.

"I'm just glad they did," Officer Marlowe said. "I'm excited to see the Ghost Eliminators at work. Since they're local 'celebrities.'" She made air quotes. "I've heard a lot about those guys."

Oscar looked at Walt with a quizzical expression.

"I may have added a line about them being celebrities," Walt admitted. It hadn't been in the script she and Oscar had gone over. "I wanted her to come!"

Oscar clicked his beak approvingly. "Very effective."

"Well, you're welcome to join us," Mrs. Third Floor said awkwardly. "The more the merrier."

"The more the merrier, huh?" Mr. Slick Hair stood in the doorway with a forced grin on his face. The Bald Guy stood behind him. "Who are we talking about here?"

"Oh, you surprised me!" Mrs. Third Floor looked

guilty, like she'd been caught stealing french fries from the table. "We were just talking to Off—"

"Carmen. Carmen Marlowe," Officer Marlowe said, stepping forward and offering her hand. "I'm just a friend. Couldn't pass up a chance to meet the famous ghost inspectors!" She shot a warning glance at Mrs. Third Floor and Mrs. Food.

"Right! This is our friend, Carmen," Mrs. Food said. She nudged Madison in the side.

"Right, Carmen's the best," Madison said cheerily. "We totally invited her."

"That's not a problem, is it?" Mrs. Food blinked innocently at Mr. Slick Hair.

Mr. Slick Hair frowned at the Bald Guy. "Well . . ."

The Bald Guy gave Officer Marlowe an appraising look. He didn't seem to like what he saw. "What Johnny is trying to say is that it's great to meet you. We'd be happy to autograph whatever. But unfortunately we're going to have to disappoint you here. Sorry." He hoisted the bag over his shoulder and turned to leave.

"What do you mean?" Officer Marlowe didn't seem to like what she saw either. Butterbean looked from one to the other. It might be time to take cover under the sofa. (That was her go-to spot. Unfortunately, she wasn't quite able to fit underneath.)

Mr. Slick Hair managed an oily smile. "What he means is, this case is very difficult, and we think it might be too dangerous for observers."

"We're going to be handling this one alone, so you ladies can sit tight down here while we take care of business," the Bald Guy said brusquely. "We'll let you know when we've finished up."

Officer Marlowe smiled at him. "I don't think so," she said. "I'm familiar with your show. Homeowners are there a lot. It doesn't seem particularly dangerous. Is there something you don't want us to see?"

The ghost men exchanged a quick glance. "No! Not at all. This is a pretty standard haunting," Mr. Slick Hair said.

"Severe, but nothing that unusual," the Bald Guy said.

"But nothing sensitive ladies like yourselves need to see," Mr. Slick Hair finished.

Officer Marlowe snorted. "Then there shouldn't be a problem having us observe," she said. "We can take it. Come on, 'ladies.'" She started toward the door.

"Right, just let me get one thing," Mrs. Third Floor said, making her move toward Walt. Walt's eyes widened, and she braced herself, tensing up her stomach muscles. That lady had not learned one thing about holding animals.

"Whoa, whoa there, ladies," Mr. Slick Hair said. "We need a little time to set up."

"What is there to set up?" Officer Marlowe folded her arms.

"Camera, EMF equipment, sensors, that kind of thing," the Bald Guy said. "Drink your coffee. We'll let you know when we're ready."

Officer Marlowe narrowed her eyes but nodded. "We'll give you fifteen minutes." She set a timer on her watch.

"Got it," the Bald Guy said, bumping into Mr. Slick Hair in their rush to get upstairs.

Officer Marlowe watched them go. Then she turned to Mrs. Third Floor. "Too bad. I'd be very interested in seeing what they're doing up there."

"Me too," Walt said. She looked back at Wallace. "Rats?"

"Got it," Wallace said, nodding toward Marco and Polo.

Without a word, the rats silently slipped out of their cage and disappeared into the vents.

"What is THAT supposed to be?" Marco and Polo peered out into the living room of Apartment 5B. Marco and Polo had gone into the upper vents while

Wallace had gone to the lower vent behind the couch. They figured that was the best way not to miss anything. "Is that a GHOST?"

The Bald Guy had finished setting up the camera and had taken what looked like a gauzy pile of laundry out of his bag. He went down the hallway and ducked into one of the bedrooms just as Mr. Slick Hair hurried in with a big piece of what looked like Plexiglas.

"What is THAT supposed to be?" Marco said again. "And what is he doing in the bedroom?"

"We should check," Polo said to Marco. "We need to figure this out."

"Oh, don't worry—it's all clear now," the white cat

said. Marco and Polo jumped, bruising their noses on the vent grate.

The white cat burst out in a gale of laughter. "GET IT? It's PLEXIGLAS, and I said it's ALL CLEAR NOW." She nudged Marco in the ribs and then sighed. "I kill myself. My talent is so wasted on rats like you."

"What are you even DOING HERE?" Marco gasped. The cat freaked him out more than he liked to admit.

"Aren't you supposed to be getting ready?" Polo demanded. "They'll be here ANY MINUTE."

"Oh, I've got plenty of time." The white cat wiped her eyes and let out one last giggle. "But if they're pulling this trick, your Mrs. Third Floor is in for a fright. I've seen this one before."

"What? You have?" Marco pressed his face onto the vent to look into the living room. He could just make out Wallace near the edge of the couch below. "WALLACE!" he shrieked. "DID YOU HEAR THAT? SHE'S SEEN THIS BEFORE!"

"WHAT?" Wallace said, cupping his ear. Marco could be a little shrill when he screamed like that.

"Ask him if they're hanging that cloth thing up in the bedroom." The white cat lounged dramatically next to the vent. (Well, she did the best she could. It was a tight squeeze.)

"TELL US WHAT THEY'RE DOING!" Polo yelled down at Wallace.

He nodded at her and then hurried after the two men. He made the trip in short bursts—from the couch to the chair, from the chair to the table, and then to the entrance of the hallway. He edged slowly along the hallway wall until he could peek inside the room.

He reeled back. "Holy cow!" he squeaked. He turned and raced back to the couch in one move. There was no time to do the slow route.

"WHAT WAS IT?" Marco yelled, but Wallace ignored him. He just streaked right back under the couch and disappeared.

"Well, that doesn't seem good," Polo said, craning her neck to get a better look. She'd expected Wallace to say something. "Where did he go?"

A few seconds later they had the answer. Wallace shot up into the vent and collapsed at their feet. "Guys! That thing in there, it's a ghost! They were hanging a ghost up on the ceiling!"

"Exactly," the white cat purred. "Classic. Just what I thought." She shrugged. "Well, you have to hand it to these guys, they know their business."

"What do you mean?" Marco was pretty sure their business was scamming old ladies.

"It's just a little something called Pepper's Ghost," the white cat said. "I've seen it many times." She gave Marco a bashful look. "You may not know this, but when I was a kitten, I was known to pop out of a top hat every now and then."

Three rats blinked at her.

"What?" Marco finally said.

"It's a famous illusion," she sighed. "An old magician's trick. They set up the ghost dummy, or a person hides, whatever you want. Then you fix the Plexiglas and lights just so, and voilà! Ghost appears." She looked at them sympathetically. "I'm sorry to say, but they're going to scare the pants off your humans."

"Not if we scare them first," Wallace said, clenching his fists. He pressed his face up to the vent opening and scanned the room. He could just see Mr. Slick Hair setting up the Plexiglas. "JEROME! CHAD! You guys there?"

Jerome oozed out of the sink and waved lazily. "Naturally. What did you all decide? Are we going for scares or professional ruin?"

"BOTH!" Wallace yelled. "FULL STEAM AHEAD."

Jerome smiled. "Excellent." He waved a tentacle in the direction of the countertop. "Chad? Camera, please."

A spot on the counter flickered and turned into a gray octopus. With a nod, Chad slid down the cabinets onto the floor.

Polo shuddered. "Heck, we don't even need a fake ghost. That would scare Mrs. Third Floor right there."

Marco didn't argue. He'd never gotten used to Chad's cloaking abilities.

Jerome cleared his throat. "One last thing. Would you all mind if I had a little fun? So to speak? I have an idea."

Wallace's eyes narrowed. "Go for it." As far as he was concerned, nothing was off the table anymore.

"GOODY!" Jerome clapped his tentacles together. "This is going to be FUN!" He disappeared back into the sink.

Chad had reached the tripod and pulled himself up to the camera. With a quick flick of the tentacle, he hit the record switch. Then he gave the octopus equivalent of a thumbs-up and slid back down the pole.

It was just in time, too. Mr. Slick Hair was coming down the hallway into the room. He barely missed stepping on one of Chad's tentacles. Chad quickly camouflaged himself, but before he did, Polo saw a look of pure rage cross his face. Mr. Slick Hair didn't know what he was in for.

"How much time do we have?" Mr. Slick Hair

called into the bedroom. "We should've just gotten the money and ditched the old lady. I don't trust this new friend of hers."

The Bald Guy came in. "Me neither. I swear I've seen that chick somewhere before. But stop stressing. We'll be fine. I could do this setup in my sleep. Plexiglas in place?"

"All set," Mr. Slick Hair said with a smirk.

The Bald Guy nodded in approval. "Good. The dry ice is down, lights are all set . . . we're good to go." He slapped Mr. Slick Hair on the back. "Trust me, those ladies will only last a minute before they run screaming downstairs. Then we break everything down, tell her the ghost is gone, and we're out of here. This way we get our money, and she has nothing but good things to say about us." He held out his fist for a fist bump. "Showtime?"

"Showtime," Mr. Slick Hair said, bumping fists.

Wallace's eyes gleamed. "Showtime."

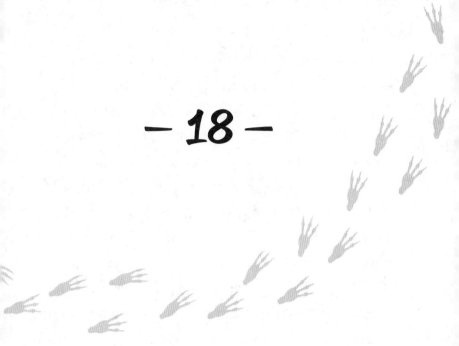

– 18 –

"WHAT'S WITH THE LIGHTS IN HERE?" OFFICER Marlowe stood in the doorway looking around Apartment 5B. "Did a bulb blow out?"

Mr. Slick Hair ushered her inside. "I'm afraid the ghost is not pleased that we're here," he said in a low voice. "It's hoping to drive us out with its negative energy. Three bulbs exploded while we were setting up our equipment." He put a hand on Mrs. Third Floor's shoulder, startling her so much she almost hit the ceiling. "I'm afraid we may be in for a bad time today. I tried to warn you." He glared at Officer Marlowe.

"I'll be okay," Mrs. Third Floor said. "I have the cat with me." She hoisted up Walt, who was dangling from her arms. "And Madison has the dog."

Madison silently held up the leash as evidence.

Walt gurgled.

"Well, let's get going. Quiet, please." Mr. Slick Hair raised his hands and threw his head back. "SPIRITS! YOU MUST LEAVE THIS PLACE! I COMMAND YOU!"

There was an eerie silence. Butterbean looked around. There didn't seem to be any evidence of spirits, either leaving or staying put. She nudged Walt's hanging foot. "Go time?" she wuffled softly.

Mrs. Third Floor shivered and hugged Walt more tightly.

Walt looked up at the vent. A little rat arm stuck out and gave her a thumbs-up.

Walt took a deep breath. "Plan Number One, GO!"

ᚴᛖᚴᚴᚴᛖ ᚴᛖᚴᚴᛖᚴᚴᛖ ᛖᚴᚴᚴᛖ ᚴᛖᚴᚴᛖᚴᚴᛖ

Oscar scrambled up the vent to the fifth floor. It had been very inconvenient, having to wait until the humans left before he could go into the vents. He just hoped he wasn't too late.

He could hear Walt's command as he crawled out into the open. (Luckily, no one was watching him.

His feet slipped out from under him three times. It was very undignified.)

He hurried up beside Polo and looked out into the apartment. "What's happening? Is it me yet?"

"They've set up all kinds of fake tricks. You should've seen them. But we're onto them." She grinned. "It's going to be awesome."

Marco pointed into the living room. "This is you, Oscar. Go time."

Oscar shook himself to loosen up. Then he took a deep breath and started to sing.

Butterbean felt the fur on the back of her neck start to rise. She wouldn't call Oscar a good singer, but whatever he was singing was very effective. It definitely didn't sound quite human, but it didn't sound like a bird, either. She raised her head and started to howl.

"Butterbean! Shhh!" Madison bent down and shushed her. "You're supposed to be keeping your eyes open, remember?" Butterbean made a face. She couldn't help herself. As the white cat had said, there was nothing wrong with a little improvising.

"Walt, psst!" Butterbean called. The fur on her neck was starting to prickle again. "What is that song?" She cocked her head to listen better.

"Doesn't matter! Stick to the plan," Walt gurgled. To be honest, Walt wasn't sure what song it was. At first she'd thought Oscar was doing a country number, but now she was getting more of an "Itsy Bitsy Spider" kind of feeling. But whatever it was, it was perfect. Oscar was totally creeping her out.

"What is that?" Madison asked, looking around. "Do you hear that?"

Mrs. Food had a frozen expression on her face, and Mrs. Third Floor had started to whimper. Even Mr. Slick Hair looked shaken. He raised his arms a little higher. "SPIRITS! WE KNOW YOU'RE HERE."

Butterbean raised her head to howl again, but as she opened her mouth, she caught Walt's eye. Walt jerked her head in the direction of the living room. Butterbean nodded, apologetic.

She'd let herself get distracted by Oscar's singing. She shook a little to get herself into character. (Her character was Dog Freaked Out by Ghost. She'd been practicing ever since she'd gotten the part a few hours ago. The white cat had given her a couple of pointers.) Taking a deep breath, she stared at a fixed point in the middle of the room and started to whine. (The fixed point she chose was a piece of fluff on the carpet. She would totally eat it later.)

"What is it, Bean?" Madison asked in a low voice.

"What's wrong with you?" Butterbean ignored her and whined again.

"I think the dog senses something," Mrs. Third Floor said.

Mr. Slick Hair stared at Butterbean with a confused expression. She was not part of his plan. "Um. Yes, exactly." He stared at her for a few seconds more and then shrugged. "GHOSTLY SPIRITS! EVEN THE DOG SENSES YOUR PRESENCE! MAKE YOURSELF KNOWN!" He looked around for the Bald Guy. "Gord!" he hissed.

The Bald Guy nodded.

Suddenly a low eerie noise filled the apartment. Walt swiveled her ears. It was coming from the Bald Guy's jacket pocket. She glared at him.

"Look! Over there!" Mr. Slick Hair pointed down the hallway, his finger trembling. "THE GHOST IS APPEARING!"

Tendrils of vapor were gathering in the hallway near the bedroom. Mrs. Third Floor gasped and clutched Mrs. Food, who clutched Madison.

Officer Marlowe frowned.

There, in the hallway, a ghostly apparition appeared. It was transparent, but had a roughly human shape and hung suspended in the air, swaying slightly.

Butterbean yelped.

Mrs. Third Floor gave a shrill scream.

"WE HAVE ANGERED THE SPIRITS!" Mr. Slick Hair yelled. "IT'S COMING FOR YOU!" He pointed at Mrs. Third Floor.

Mrs. Third Floor was trembling so much that Walt felt like she was going to be sick. But suddenly, Mrs. Third Floor went still. She tilted her head and looked down the hallway, blinking.

Because just as suddenly as the ghost had appeared, it disappeared.

"Where did it . . ." She trailed off, looking around wildly and clutching Walt even tighter.

"It . . . uh . . ." Mr. Slick Hair shot a nasty look at the Bald Guy, who nodded in response. "IT IS DIS-PLEASED," Mr. Slick Hair continued in a booming voice. The Bald Guy edged back toward the hallway, trying to look invisible. But before he got there, he stopped short.

Because the ghostly apparition they'd seen before had been replaced by something much more terrifying.

A huge shape loomed in the hallway, a shape with multiple arms that waved and reached out toward them.

"OH NO NO NO," Mrs. Third Floor whimpered, and buried her face in Mrs. Food's shoulder.

"PSST, Walt!" Butterbean hissed. "Am I still supposed to be looking at my fixed spot, or can I look at— WHAT THE HECK? IS THAT MR. WIGGLES?" Butterbean barked.

That's when they heard the scream. It was the most bone-chilling sound any of them could ever remember hearing. And it was coming from Mr. Slick Hair.

He'd collapsed in a heap on the floor and was scrambling crab-style away from the thing in the hallway. "WHAT IS THAT?" he shrieked, pointing toward the flailing ghostly tendrils. "Gord, what have you done?"

"NOT ME!" the Bald Guy wailed, flattening himself against the wall. "I didn't do anything like that thing! Mine was just gauze!"

A ghostly tentacle reached out in his direction, and he scrambled back into the kitchen. Then he screamed and pointed at the floor. "NOOOOO!"

Everyone peered into the kitchen. Tiny white footprints had appeared on the linoleum. "Those weren't there before!" the Bald Guy screamed. "I SWEAR!"

A tentacle dangled down from the light fixture and gently touched Mr. Slick Hair on the back of the neck. (There were also some quiet giggling sounds, but no one noticed them over all the screaming.)

Mr. Slick Hair jumped away, screaming and slapping at his head. "IT TOUCHED ME! THE GHOST TOUCHED ME?"

"All right, what is this?" Officer Marlowe demanded. She'd seen just about enough.

"Don't let it get me!" Mr. Slick Hair threw himself onto the floor, grabbing at her legs for protection. She shook him off and started walking carefully down the hallway toward the ghost.

As she reached for the light switch, she smacked into the piece of Plexiglas. "Interesting," she said, smacking it again with her hand. The multi-armed ghost quickly pulled itself up and disappeared.

"Want to explain this?" She peered into the bedroom doorway. "Nice trick, guys." She went into the room, emerging a few minutes later holding the wadded-up-fabric ghost figure. "I think I see what's going on here."

Mr. Slick Hair scrambled to his feet. "No, I mean,

yes, that's a fake. We were trying to trick her, I confess. That was a scam, sure. But that thing? With the . . ." He shuddered. ". . . the . . . the arms? We didn't do that! That was a real ghost. Listen! Those noises? That's not us!"

They all listened. Oscar had stopped singing, but a new sound had started. It was one that all the animals recognized. The sound of vocal exercises.

"That's not a human sound, Officer," Mrs. Third Floor said softly.

"Officer?" Mr. Slick Hair stared up at Officer Marlowe in horror. "Wait, what? I mean, no, this was all a . . . a prank!"

"Yes, good fun," the Bald Guy said from his perch on a kitchen stool. "Just a joke between friends. Now let me out of here."

He hopped from the stool onto the couch and then scrambled over the coffee table toward the door, like he thought the ghost would grab his feet.

Officer Marlowe stepped in front of the exit, blocking the Bald Guy's path. She turned to Mrs. Third Floor. "Ma'am, I'm sorry to say these men are scamming you. This ghost? It's all fake." She put one hand to her temple. "I'm seeing a whole lot of fraud charges in their futures." She reached into her waistband and pulled out a pair of handcuffs. "I'm taking them in."

Mrs. Third Floor nodded. "Yes, you're right. I know you're right, but still . . ." She swallowed. "These men didn't vandalize the apartment. Or lick the cupcakes. They may be scammers, but there's still a ghost. Can't you hear it?"

"Cat! That's your cue!" Wallace hissed from the vent.

"I realize that, ma'am, but—"

Officer Marlowe was cut short. Because at that moment, the white cat made her appearance.

Trotting in from the kitchen, covered with flour, she gave a pathetic unearthly yowl and collapsed in a heap on the living room floor. She had even managed to find a spotlight. (It was very dramatic.)

"This is my favorite death scene," she said in between screeches and moans. She put a paw onto her forehead and fell back. "Observe my skills," she said, coughing gently and batting her eyes up at Mrs. Third

Floor. "You don't see a performance like this every day," she moaned. "OH WOE IS ME!"

"Oh, it's a kitty!" Mrs. Third Floor squealed.

"It's covered with gross stuff. What is that?" Madison said, taking a step forward to examine it. Butterbean was way ahead of her.

She snuffled at the white cat for a moment.

"Stop it! You're ruining my scene!" the cat screeched, batting at Butterbean's face before collapsing back in a heap. "OH WOE!"

Butterbean lifted a white nose and sneezed. A puff of flour flew up around them.

Madison examined Butterbean's face. "It's flour!" She stood up. "Just like before!" She did a discreet fist pump in the air. "I KNEW it wasn't a ghost! High five, dog!" She held up her hand for a high five. Butterbean did her best to high-five back.

"The poor little kitty!" Mrs. Third Floor let go of Walt, who fell in a heap on the floor. Then she scooped up the white cat and cuddled it to her chest. She didn't even notice the flour all over her front.

"There's your ghost," Officer Marlowe said, picking up the phone and pointing at the white cat with it. "I knew there was a rational explanation. That cat's been in your apartment."

Madison frowned. "But that doesn't explain the—"

"Hsst," Mrs. Food hissed, poking her in the side.

". . . pizza," Madison finished under her breath. She exchanged significant looks with Mrs. Food. "Right, that's it! That kitten must've gotten stuck in here somehow. Wow, crazy, right?"

"That cat must've licked your cupcakes," Mrs. Food said to Mrs. Third Floor.

"Poor little darling," Mrs. Third Floor cooed. "Poor baby kitten. We have to find your mommy and daddy."

"Kitten, my butt," Walt grumbled, standing up and smoothing her sweaty, matted fur. "That cat is older than me."

"I need backup at the Strathmore Building," Officer Marlowe said into the phone. Then she pointed it at the couch. "I'll need you two gentlemen to sit down there. Your little con is over."

The ghost men sat down on the couch obediently. Mr. Slick Hair was still shaking and staring at the floor. The Bald Guy had his head in his hands.

They didn't hear the cheers coming from the vent overhead or see the two octopuses high-fiving in the light fixture.

— 19 —

It didn't take Officer Travis long to show up to assist with the arrest. And he seemed very relieved to find out that the exploding flour canister episode from before had a kitten-related explanation.

"I figured it was a cat or something," he said to Mrs. Third Floor as he put the handcuffs on Mr. Slick Hair. "I said to myself, 'That's a cat doing this, not a ghost.' That's what I thought, anyway."

"Kitty kitty," Mrs. Third Floor said, cuddling the white cat. "Little sweetie pie."

"Really?" Madison said, eyeing Officer Travis skeptically. "If that's what you thought, why didn't you say so?"

Officer Travis shrugged. "Thought it was obvious."

He hustled Mr. Slick Hair away without meeting Madison's eye.

"How long is this scene, anyway?" the white cat meowed to Walt as Mrs. Third Floor made kissy noises at her. "I don't do extended runs."

Walt just smirked.

Officer Marlowe came over to Mrs. Third Floor, with Bob the maintenance man behind her. He stopped short when he saw Butterbean and Walt.

"Oh. You guys," he said, looking from Butterbean to Walt and back again. "I should've known."

They'd had some run-ins with Bob before. Butterbean lolled her tongue as a hello gesture. He didn't seem to appreciate it.

Officer Marlowe snorted. "Hello? Not them. This is the cat here," she said, pointing to the floury mess in Mrs. Third Floor's arms. "Those other animals are all accounted for."

"Right," Bob growled. "Of course. Those guys always have a cover story."

Butterbean wagged her tail at him. He ignored her.

Bob leaned forward and carefully examined the white cat, who preened like she was having hair and makeup done. Bob stepped back, dusting his hands off. "Yeah, I've seen this cat before. How'd she get in?"

"We're not sure," Officer Marlowe said. "We'll

leave that mystery for you to solve. Now if you can just get this cat home? I think she's done enough damage here."

"Did you hear that?" the white cat smirked. "They totally bought my performance."

Walt rolled her eyes.

Bob looked at his clipboard. "So I'm thinking this cat lives next door." He flipped the papers back down on the clipboard and reached out for the white cat. "Come on, Bertha. Let's get you home."

Butterbean's jaw dropped. "Bertha? Your name's BERTHA?"

"PRINCESS JUBILEE! CALL ME PRINCESS JUBILEE!" the cat shrieked as Bob carried her away. "Princess Jubilee's my stage name! No one calls me BERTHA!"

"Wow. I didn't expect that," Butterbean said to Walt.

Walt snickered. "Princess Jubilee." It was almost worse than Bertha.

"Well, that's that," Officer Marlowe said, coming over to Mrs. Third Floor. "I'm heading down to the precinct. I'll be back later to take your statements." She held up the video camera. "Evidence. Those doofuses taped the whole thing—set up, crime, confession, you name it." She shook her head again and looked down at Butterbean. "I'm just surprised those animals of yours didn't root out that cat right away. You'd think they would've tipped us off to a strange animal."

Mrs. Food frowned down at Butterbean, who blinked back with her most innocent face on. "Hmm. Yes, you'd think." She turned to Madison. "I'm going to be a while here. Could you put them back in the apartment? I think they're overtired. Especially Bean, with all that howling."

"I was in character!" Butterbean complained as Madison dragged her to the elevator.

She didn't stop grumbling until Madison unlocked the door to Mrs. Food's apartment a few minutes later.

"Well, I'm glad that's over," Butterbean said to Walt as Madison shut them back inside.

"But it isn't over, is it?" a voice said as the door closed behind them.

Butterbean stopped short. Sitting in the middle of the sofa, waiting for them, was Jerome.

He drummed his tentacles on the arm of the sofa. "Well, I did my part. Now how are you getting me home?"

Luckily, Jerome was in a much better mood once Oscar appealed to his better nature. (The way to appeal to Jerome's better nature was with sardines. Lots of sardines.)

"So you think you can get me a map of the pipes?" Jerome said, spraying a fine mist of fish juice. "Since I obviously can't go back the way I came."

"Right," Walt said. "The city website is sure to have one. Once we get you that map, you can just follow the pipes back to the zoo."

"And take Larry down," Jerome growled menacingly. (Or as menacingly as he could with a mouth full of sardines.) "I'll be so entertaining, they'll never even THINK about replacing me."

"YEAH!" Butterbean cheered, high-fiving one of Jerome's free tentacles. She was still hyped up from the ghost stuff earlier.

"We think it should be pretty straightforward," Oscar said, scooting down the arm of the sofa. He was definitely going to need a bath to wash off all the fish residue.

"Good. Because I don't want to end up in some water recycling plant or decorative fountain or something," Jerome grumbled. He shook his fist again. "TAKE LARRY DOWN!"

"TAKE HIM DOWN!" Marco and Polo cheered. The enthusiasm was a little contagious.

Jerome giggled and elbowed Wallace in the side. "Did you hear those ghost guys scream? Oh man, I should incorporate that ghost stuff into my routine at the zoo. It'll be a huge draw. Seriously, you guys have given me a lot of great new ideas." He tapped his cheek thoughtfully. "I think I just needed this quality time away from the paparazzi to find myself again. You know, personal growth and all that."

"Erm. Great," Oscar said, eyeing the door. Mrs. Food and Madison could get back any minute, and they still had to use the computer. "We're glad it was beneficial. But maybe you should go get your things together?"

"Right," Jerome sighed, flipping the empty sardine container toward the trash can. (It missed.) "No point in wasting more time here." He stretched and headed off to the kitchen. "I'll be hanging at Chad's place until you get that map. He's going to be crushed that I'm leaving."

Jerome climbed up onto the counter and paused. "You know, those pipes run both ways. You ever want to pull a prank like that again, I'm your octopus. You got it?"

"Got it," Walt said solemnly.

Jerome waved a tentacle at each of them like he was doing a fancy interpretive dance and then disappeared down the drain.

Oscar looked at Walt nervously. "I just hope you're right about that map."

Walt's whisker twitched. "I hope so too."

They were not right about the map. Walt had been searching for the past ten minutes with no luck. And Mrs. Food wouldn't be gone much longer.

"Well?" Oscar said, tapping his feet impatiently.

"Anything?" Butterbean asked, her nose trembling.

Walt shook her head. "Nothing." The city waterworks website seemed to be woefully inadequate.

"This is ridiculous," Oscar said bitterly. "Why is there no easily accessible map? What about regular citizens who need to know how to get somewhere by pipe? What about them?"

"Yeah, what about them?" Butterbean echoed. She had a feeling there wasn't much demand for pipe maps in human circles, but she wanted to be supportive.

Walt kept typing. "The public site just doesn't have the plans,

and the section with the documents is password protected," Walt explained. "Very securely password protected. I can't even see what's there."

"I wish he could just go back the way he got here!" Polo complained. "That would be so much easier!"

"Yes, well, we all do," Oscar said. "But that's obviously not an option."

They all stared at the computer screen for a long minute.

"Why don't you hack it?" Marco finally called from the doorway. He was officially the lookout, but he kept getting distracted. Whatever was happening with the computer sounded a lot more interesting than watching an empty living room. "You know, the computer. Hack it up."

"Yes! Let's hack it up!" Butterbean said. "That sounds like fun!"

"Ooh good idea, I'll hack it," Walt said sarcastically.

Marco looked wounded. It didn't sound like Walt was being serious. "Maybe just a couple of hacks?"

Walt slumped a little. "I'm sorry. I tried hacking. I can't crack it. The website has a two-part authentication system, and I don't have a security fob."

"Yeah. Wow," Marco said. "That stinks." He didn't have any idea what any of that meant.

"Can you get one?" Polo asked. She wasn't sure

what a security fob was, but how hard could it be?

Pretty hard, apparently.

"Doubtful. I'm not a city employee, and they're the only ones who get them. Is there anyone in this building who has one, Butterbean? I'm sure Chad would be able to 'borrow' it for us." She didn't even bother to make the air quotes. They all knew what it meant when Chad borrowed things.

Butterbean sat down and stared at the ceiling while she went through her mental list of the residents of the building. Her lips moved while she thought. Finally, she made a face. "I don't think so."

"High Heel Woman? Spicy Food Couple? Mrs. Hates Dogs?" Oscar said. Surely there was someone.

"No. Sorry," Butterbean said.

"Man Who Smokes Cigars?" Walt said. "None of them?"

Butterbean shook her head. "High Heel Woman works in a store, I think, cosmetics section. Man Who Smokes Cigars is a bank guy. Mrs. Hates Dogs is retired, and Spicy Food Couple does something on the internet. A food blob? Something like that. The only office person I remember smelling was Man Who Smelled Like Onions, but he's gone."

"And there isn't any other way to get the plans?" Oscar asked Walt.

"There's one other way," Walt said slowly. "We could fill out a request form. Then they'd send them to us."

"Oh!" Butterbean said. "Let's do that, then!"

Walt shook her head. "It wouldn't work."

"Will they send them in the mail? Is that the problem?" Oscar wasn't willing to give up. "I know tampering with the mail is a federal crime, but we've never let that stop us before, right? We can certainly find a way to intercept the plans before Mrs. Food sees them." They'd planned a heist. Surely it wouldn't be that hard to steal a letter.

"That's not it," Walt explained. "It takes four to six weeks. Processing."

"Oh." Butterbean sat down hard. Oscar's feathers drooped.

Four to six weeks was a long time. Four to six weeks of Jerome was even longer.

"We'll find another way," Oscar said. They'd have to.

When Mrs. Food and Madison got back, they found the animals lying lethargically around the living room. No matter how much brainstorming the animals had done, they hadn't been able to find another way.

Walt had draped herself along the back of the couch.

Butterbean was partially wedged under the coffee table. Marco and Polo were lying flat on the floor of their aquarium. And Oscar was sitting gloomily on the bottom of his cage. (Wallace was lying behind the couch, but Mrs. Food and Madison didn't notice him.) They had failed. And they hadn't told Jerome.

"What's wrong, guys? Too much ghosty stuff for you?" Madison asked, patting Walt on the head. Walt twitched an ear in response.

Madison bent down to look under the coffee table. "Butterbean, we did it! We stopped those guys! Aren't you excited?" Butterbean didn't even move. Madison stood up. "I think they're traumatized," she told Mrs. Food.

"They'll stop being traumatized when I get the can opener out," Mrs. Food scoffed, going into the kitchen.

"We're being depressed," Butterbean said without moving. She'd thought it was pretty obvious. They'd run out of ideas. They would never get Jerome back to the zoo now. They were stuck with him.

Madison picked up the remote. "Maybe we can watch the news? They like that." She sat down on the couch and rested her head on Walt's back. "Want to see the news, cat?"

Walt didn't respond.

It didn't matter anyway. The News was over.

"Oh crud," Madison said, turning the TV off again. "I was hoping they'd say something about that new octopus. I still can't believe Mr. Wiggles is really gone!"

"Well, it's been a while," Mrs. Food said, setting the table. "They can't keep looking forever."

"I know, but I was right there!" Madison said, getting up. "I was probably one of the last people to see him!"

"Last person," Butterbean couldn't help saying. "You were the last person. I've told you that A MILLION TIMES."

"Maybe even the LAST person," Madison said.

"Thank you," Butterbean said.

"I just keep thinking about it, you know, trying to retrace my steps in my head. Surely I saw something, right? Maybe something I saw is the key to everything! It's like one of those mystery movies where they call everybody into the drawing room to reveal the killer."

"Right," Mrs. Food said. "Madison, help me with the rice, okay?"

"Sure," Madison said, going into the kitchen.

None of the animals moved. Then slowly, Walt's ears started to perk up.

"Oscar," she said without moving. Her voice was muffled by the couch cushion. "Did you hear what she said?"

"I did," Oscar said.

"Are you thinking what I'm thinking?"

Oscar sat up a little straighter. "About the murder mystery?"

"The drawing room part? Calling everyone together? Retracing steps?"

"Exactly." Oscar shot up onto his perch. "How much time do you need?"

Walt jumped down from the cushion. "Not long. Cover for me, Bean!"

She streaked into the office.

Butterbean sat up in confusion. She was not thinking what they were thinking. "WHAT'S HAPPENING?" she barked, and then started running in circles around the living room. She didn't have time to come up with a new distraction technique. Circles were always her best option.

"What in the world?" Mrs. Food came out into the living room.

Madison poked her head around the corner. "She's lost it." Then she frowned. "What is that cat doing?" She wiped her hands on a dish towel and headed off into the office.

"OH NOOOOOOOO," Butterbean wailed. She couldn't even manage a simple distraction anymore.

Madison was back less than a minute later. "She's

playing with the computer keyboard. It's like she thinks she can type," she laughed.

Butterbean and Oscar exchanged glances. As long as Mrs. Food and Madison thought Walt's computer hijinks were all a big joke, they should be okay. Just as long as they didn't investigate too much.

Walt stalked in a few minutes later and sat down in the middle of the living room, a smug expression on her face.

"Did it work?" Butterbean asked, collapsing in a heap next to her.

"Just wait." She started grooming her tail.

It wasn't long before there was a knock at the door. Mrs. Third Floor poked her head in. "Madison?" She let herself in. "Sorry to bother you, but I just got the STRANGEST message that I think was meant for you. It was someone from the City Zoo. They need you to come by tomorrow for some kind of reenactment? It's part of the Wiggles investigation. Anyway, I wrote down what they said." She handed a piece of paper to Madison.

"Okay, thanks." Madison looked at the piece of paper. "Huh."

Walt smoothed her whiskers. "Bingo."

− 20 −

"MADISON, COME QUICK!" MRS. FOOD HIT THE pause button on the Television as Madison came into the apartment. "Look! He's back! Mr. Wiggles is back!"

"What?" Madison dumped her book bag onto the entryway floor, her water bottle bouncing out into the dining room.

Walt inspected it carefully. She was just glad it was empty this time.

"No way! I was JUST THERE! When did this happen?" Madison said, sitting down on the couch.

"They just announced it," Mrs. Food said. "Here, I'll run it back."

Mrs. Food rewound for a few seconds and then hit play.

"And he's back! Just as mysteriously as Mr. Wiggles disappeared, today he returned with no explanation. Zoo officials say they had almost given up hope of ever seeing the beloved celebrity and spokes-octopus again, but today he mysteriously reappeared in his own tank, ringing the bell that tells zookeepers that he wants a snack. Zoo officials say he seems healthy and happy, and may have even put on a little weight."

"He did eat a LOT," Butterbean whispered to Walt.

The camera zoomed in on the tank holding Mr. Wiggles. He pulled himself up and waved to the camera, spitting water onto the reporter standing nearby. Then he winked and gave the camera a thumbs-up.

"Did you see that?" Butterbean gasped. "He winked at us!"

"It wasn't necessarily at us, Butterbean," Oscar said. But he secretly thought it was.

"Zoo officials say this is especially good news in light of the recent scandal involving European octopus Monsieur Octavio, also known as the Annihilator. Back to you, Herb," the reporter said, trying to ignore the water dripping down her nose.

"That is good news! And boy did they dodge a bullet with that Annihilator. Talk about bad news!" The anchorman chuckled to himself. "Glad to see that Wiggles character back where he belongs."

Mrs. Food hit pause. "What's all this about the Annihilator?"

Madison grinned. "You didn't hear about that? He escaped from his tank and ate the entire display of saltwater fish. Apparently he does that a lot. That's why they were trying to get rid of him."

Mrs. Food smiled and got up. "Well, then, I'm glad their reenactment worked. You can be proud that you helped find him."

"No, but that's just it. It didn't work!" Madison said, a confused expression on her face. "It was the weirdest thing. There was no official reenactment at all—they didn't even know what I was talking about! So I walked around and did the stuff I did before, but it felt kind of dumb, so I just came home."

Mrs. Food looked confused. "But the phone call—"

"I know!" Madison said.

"Huh," Mrs. Food said thoughtfully.

They both stared at the pets for a long second. Butterbean tried not to squirm. There was no way they could pin this on them.

"Anyway, it was strange . . ." Madison said, shrugging.

Mrs. Food frowned. "This will sound silly, but you don't think—"

"YOOHOO!" a voice came from the front entrance. Mrs. Third Floor was standing in the doorway. "Beulah, Madison, I need help, please!"

"Oh no, not again," Mrs. Food muttered as she hurried to the door. "What is it, Mildred? What can I do?"

Mrs. Third Floor laughed. "You can give me my spare key. You'll never believe it. I found a renter!"

"Already?" Mrs. Food gasped, handing her the key.

"Already?" Wallace groaned from his pile of cedar chips. He knew it was too good to last.

Mrs. Third Floor clasped her hands together. "Yes, and I didn't even have to list it. You're going to be so surprised. Meet my new tenant!" She stepped aside and held her arms out like she was displaying a refrigerator on the Television.

Officer Marlowe poked her head around the door. "Hello, you two."

"Officer Marlowe!" Madison blurted. "You're moving in?"

"Guilty," Officer Marlowe said. "I just had to snap it up. Don't tell anyone, but I had my eye on that place from the first minute I saw it."

"And she can help protect it from ghosts!" Mrs. Third Floor said happily.

"Ghosts don't mess with me," Officer Marlowe smirked. "Mostly because I don't believe in them."

"Well, that's wonderful news," Mrs. Food said as Mrs. Third Floor held out the key. "Welcome to the

building. It would be good to have a police officer nearby."

"Thanks," Officer Marlowe said, taking the key. She turned to go and then hesitated. "Would you like to see what I'm doing with the place? Mrs. Thurfel said it was okay if I did a little decorating."

Mrs. Third Floor beamed. "I'm going to let her put nail holes in the walls AND paint the rooms a different color! I might even let her have a pet!" She cleared her throat and shot Walt and Butterbean a look. "I haven't decided about that one, though. No offense," she said to Butterbean.

"None taken," Butterbean said.

"So, what do you think, Wallace?" Walt asked, raising an eyebrow. "She might be able to have a pet."

Wallace shook his head. "No, that's okay. I'll find a new place. I was actually thinking about one on seven. That's my favorite floor, you know. That 7C is pretty nice."

"But that's where Mrs. Power Walker lives!" Butterbean gasped.

Wallace shrugged. "I know. I get the feeling she wouldn't mind. We'll see. It's just a thought."

"Come on, Beulah. We need your opinion on paint colors," Mrs. Third Floor said, hurrying into the hallway. "You too, Madison."

Madison picked up the leash. "Do you want Butterbean and Walt, too?"

Mrs. Third Floor made a face. "No, we don't need them. The ghost is gone! Besides . . ." Her voice dropped to a whisper. "I have carpeting."

"Ah," Madison said, putting the leash away. "Sorry, guys." She followed the others out.

"Offense taken," Butterbean grumbled.

"Oh please," Walt said as the door closed. "NOW she has carpeting? How insulting. 'I have carpeting.' Well, I have bruises across my rib cage, thank you very much. That's gratitude for you."

"I wouldn't pee on her carpet if she begged me," Butterbean said. (Although secretly, she wasn't so sure.)

"Let it go, Walt," Oscar said. "Think of it this way. Your dangling days are over. You're safe now."

Walt sniffed. "I guess you're right."

"Are they gone?" The white cat poked her head out from under the couch. "I thought those guys would never leave."

"Tell me about it," Chad said, slipping up the drain into the kitchen sink. "Where are the snacks? Jerome cleaned me out before he left. My entire stash of canned salmon is gone."

He jerked the refrigerator door open with one tentacle and then hung suspended between the counter and the door as he rummaged around. "Herring snacks. Perfect." He grabbed the jar of herring and swung himself back up onto the counter.

"Retirement isn't for everyone, let me tell you," the white cat said, settling down on Walt's cushion and propping her feet up. "Mr. Wiggles wouldn't have been happy staying here."

"I wouldn't have been happy with him staying here," Chad muttered, sucking down half of the herring snacks. Butterbean was impressed. (Although she didn't know how they were going to explain the missing snacks to Mrs. Food.)

"He wanted me to give you this, by the way," Chad said, flipping a piece of paper in Oscar's direction. It was a dramatically posed photo of Jerome, signed with an inky tentacle.

"An autographed photo . . ." Oscar breathed. "Just like he promised."

"You should see the outtakes," Chad snickered, spraying herring all over the counter.

"Great." Walt eyed the photo. There was definitely some retouching there. "Now, did you want someth . . ." Walt's voice trailed off. She held up a paw. "Do you hear that? What is that?" Her eyes were wide as she looked at Oscar.

He cocked his head and listened. "Oh no."

A slight splashing sound was coming from the bathroom.

"It can't be him. The water bottle was empty when she got back," Walt said. "I looked."

"Is it Chad?" Oscar asked.

"Still over here, genius." Chad waved a tentacle from the kitchen. "I can move fast, but not that fast."

Butterbean swallowed hard. "Ghost?"

"OH NO, IS THIS PLACE HAUNTED TOO?" Wallace wailed. It was so unfair.

Oscar flew over to the bathroom door, followed by the others. Slowly they pushed open the door.

"WHOOHOOO HOT TUB!" Marco cheered as he reclined in the sink. "This is the best. Do the bubbles again, Polo!"

Marco and Polo were lounging in the half-filled sink. Polo held on to the sides and kicked her feet to make bubbles.

"Nope, I'm outta here." The white cat turned and stalked back into the vent behind the couch. She'd already had one bath too many that week. Flour was a lot harder to get off than she'd expected.

"Walt, Oscar, look, it's our very own bubble bath!" Polo cheered.

"Just like Chad and Jerome had in the other place!" Marco said, splashing water at them.

"Except we don't have a Jacuzzi. We just have feet!" Polo explained.

Butterbean climbed up to sniff the water. "I'm not going to fit in there," she said, snuffling at the bubbles.

Wallace scrambled up the cabinet and slid into the water. He giggled. "Come on in, the water's fine!" he said happily. "I always wanted to say that."

Oscar landed on the edge of the sink and dangled his feet in the water.

Walt pawed gently at the water. "I'll pass, but thanks." She didn't like to get wet. But it was good to just have fun for a change and not worry about everything. Especially pesky octopuses like Jerome.

She looked up just in time to see Chad flying through the air.

"CANNONBALL!"

Acknowledgments

This book was written in 2020, which wasn't the easiest time to try to write something funny. Fortunately, I was working with some wonderful and very talented people.

Big thanks go out to Reka Simonsen, David Mottram, Kate Testerman, and everyone at Atheneum. You guys are the best.

Thanks also to:

My family, for being my sounding board (and the only people I've been within six feet of all year).

My quarantine buddy, Howdy, and her dog friends at Belmont Park (for giving her the semblance of a social life).

Kyrie O'Connor, for providing the latest in octopus news, and Peter Sagal, for his inspiring octopus anecdote.

My SCBWI friends, for being such a great support system.

The scientific and medical communities, for the light at the end of the tunnel.

And in memory of Christine Veillette. I was very lucky to know her and work with such a talented web designer.

And for providing much needed pandemic distractions, additional thanks go out to: Michael Jordan, the Championship Bulls, and the producers of *The Last Dance* documentary; Lin-Manuel Miranda and the cast of *Hamilton*; everyone involved with *Ted Lasso*; and Pashmina, Scoot, Beau, Melba, Peanut, Vesta, Broffina, Octavian, Rodney, and Ketchup, for all the sleeved aprons, relay tanks, and yodel sweaters. (I have plenty now, thanks.)